Parker was going to jump the drop.

"Last one back buys the soda," Parker said, waving as they galloped off, his bright yellow shirtsleeves rippling in the breeze. Sterling got excited again, eager to make a race of it, so Christina had to circle her two more times before continuing the course. When she looked up, Parker was already out of sight.

"Good girl," Christina said as they set off down the field in a reasonably collected hand gallop. The tension had gone out of Sterling's neck, and Christina was pleased that the mare felt lighter in her hands. As they started to pass the old hay barn with the scary drop jump, Christina caught a glimpse of yellow out of the corner of her eye. Sterling saw it, too, and swerved away.

"Oh, no," Christina muttered as she sat back in the saddle, closing her hands on the reins. The yellow disappeared around the barn. It was Parker.

"Don't!" she yelled when Foxy appeared in the far opening. But Christina knew in the pit of her stomach that it was too late. Parker was going to jump the drop.

Collect all the books in the
THOROUGHBRED series:

THOROUGHBRED Super Editions:

ASHLEIGH'S Thoroughbred Collection

*coming soon

THOROUGHBRED

RACING
PARKER

CREATED BY
JOANNA CAMPBELL

WRITTEN BY
DALE GASQUE

HarperEntertainment
A Division of HarperCollinsPublishers

HarperEntertainment
A Division of HarperCollins*Publishers*
10 East 53rd Street, New York, NY 10022-5299

Produced by 17th Street Productions,
a division of Daniel Weiss Associates, Inc.

ISBN 0-06-106562-5

First printing: March 1999

Printed in the United States of America

Visit HarperEntertainment on the World Wide Web at
http://www.harpercollins.com

❖ 10 9 8 7 6 5 4 3 2 1

With love to Charlie, Courtney, and Joe,
who are behind me all the way

"RACE YOU!" KEVIN MCLEAN'S VOICE CALLED.

Christina Reese twisted in the saddle as her friend came out of the woods and cantered up alongside her on his horse, Jasper. She could see by his teasing grin that Kevin didn't really expect her to accept his challenge.

Sterling Dream, Christina's dappled gray mare, gave a little buck of protest when she wasn't allowed to break from a trot into a canter, too. "How far?" Christina asked, her legs and hands taking a firm hold as the headstrong mare lengthened her stride to keep even with Jasper's tawny shoulder. Sterling's long Thoroughbred legs covered as much ground in a trot as the smaller Anglo-Arab's canter.

"End of the field?" Kevin suggested, standing in his stirrups as Jasper pulled at the bit.

They were on their way to Whisperwood Farm, the new sport horse breeding and training facility Kevin's older half-sister, Samantha Nelson, and her husband, Tor, were setting up. It was a nice walk along the paths between the fenced pastures and through woods dividing Kentucky's sprawling horse properties, but the open field offered a chance to do more than walk.

Christina glanced down the inviting stretch of grass before turning to Dylan Becker, who was bringing up the rear on his chestnut horse, Dakota. "I'm game if you are."

Sterling took advantage of Christina's moment of inattention and leaped into a canter. Christina grinned as the mare practically danced in place. She loved the way Sterling felt like a giant spring coiled beneath her. Even though the mare had been off the racetrack for more than six months, she was always eager to go.

"Okay, girl," Christina said, moving her hands up Sterling's neck. "You can run." Before the words were out of her mouth, Sterling shot forward with a burst of speed that left Jasper and Dakota in the dust.

"Hey! No fair," Kevin shouted. "I didn't say go."

Christina laughed as she glanced behind her. Loose strands from her strawberry blond braid whipped across her face as she watched the others try to catch up. Kevin, crouched forward like a jockey with his face inches away from Jasper's creamy mane, had a head start. Dylan sat taller in the saddle as Dakota, with his four white socks flashing, gained on them. Dakota's quarter-horse hindquarters were built to sprint.

But Sterling was bred for speed. Christina could feel her mare's shoulders stretching forward, her front legs reaching as they flew across the level ground. The wind made Christina's eyes water, but she pushed on anyway, locking her legs around Sterling's powerful body.

Too soon, the wide strip of hayed ground that separated the field from the road loomed ahead. "Okay, girl," Christina said, settling into the saddle and straightening to let Sterling know that the race was over.

Sterling's black-tipped ears flicked back, but instead of slowing, she leaned against the bit. They left the mown grass and continued across the rougher ground.

Christina caught her breath as she fought Sterling for the bit. Each stride was carrying them closer to the two-lane road. Out of the corner of her eye, Christina saw a pickup truck in the distance.

"Whoa," she said, planting her right hand on the crest of Sterling's mane and pulling her left rein sharply up and back. A pulley rein was hard on Sterling's mouth, but galloping into the road would be far worse.

Sterling's hindquarters came underneath her so abruptly that Christina thought for a second the mare was going to rear in response to the jab at her mouth. Christina quickly lowered her hand, pulling Sterling's head to the left as she drove her forward. By the time the truck rattled past them, Sterling was cantering a scant ten feet away, parallel to the hard blacktop.

"Whoa, whoa," Christina said, her words matching the rhythm of Sterling's strides. She sank deep into the saddle, her fingers squeezing and releasing the reins in a series of half-halts. Finally the mare relented, shaking her head as she dropped into a trot, then a walk. By the time Dylan and Kevin caught up, Christina was scolding Sterling.

"Crazy girl," she said, her hand reaching behind the saddle to pat Sterling's hot flank. "Did you think you were still on the racetrack or something?" Christina didn't know if it was the mare's muscles or her own that were quivering as her fingers glided over the slippery sweat that darkened Sterling's silver dapples to pewter. Sterling jigged and tossed her head as if she was ready to go again.

"Cheater," Kevin said, grinning. "You had a head start." His freckles stood out against the red flush of his cheeks.

"We would have won anyway," Christina said, flicking her braid behind her shoulder. "Sterling hasn't been able to let loose like that in a long time."

Christina was used to teasing Kevin. His father, Ian McLean, was the head trainer at Whitebrook, the Thoroughbred training and breeding farm that Christina's parents owned and operated. Christina and Kevin were almost like sister and brother, since they had run around the farm together for twelve years—ever since they were in diapers.

Dylan rode up on her other side. "Give us a heart attack, why don't you." His tone was light, but his brown eyes were serious. "When I saw that truck coming . . ."

As Dylan's voice faded, Christina's stomach fluttered. Dylan was more than just a friend to ride with. He sounded like he really cared about her.

"I'm sorry I scared you," she said. "But you don't have to worry about me. I've had a lot of practice getting run away with." She thought about how many times her pony, Trib, had grabbed the bit in his teeth and taken off with her before she'd learned how to stop him.

"He wasn't just worried about you," Kevin said, lightening the tension. "He didn't want to see a nice-looking truck banged up."

Now Dylan laughed, too. "I thought you were trying to teach Sterling *not* to run flat out like that." Dylan was teasing more than scolding.

"I know," Christina said, a little embarrassed. If Sterling was going to be a successful event horse, the mare needed to forget her racing days. Dressage, cross-country, and stadium jumping required discipline and control, not madcap speed.

But like Sterling, racing was in Christina's blood, too. Her mother, Ashleigh Griffen, was a successful jockey who had won some of the biggest races in the United States, including the Kentucky Derby. And her father, Mike Reese, had trained as many winners as

Ashleigh had ridden. Christina had grown up surrounded by Thoroughbreds in the heart of Kentucky racing country.

"You're right," Christina continued. "But it was great, wasn't it, girl?" She stretched forward and flipped a stray lock of Sterling's silver-streaked mane so that it lay properly on the right side of her neck.

"Come on, you guys," Kevin said, gathering up his reins to trot. "I want to see Sam's new stallion."

Christina did, too. Ever since Samantha moved back from Ireland she'd been talking about the Irish Thoroughbred stallion who would be the foundation of their breeding program. Like all imported stallions, the horse had been in quarantine in New York for four weeks. If all had gone as scheduled, he would have arrived at the Nelsons' farm late the previous night.

As they turned up the driveway of the farm, Christina admired the new wood sign that hung from two white chains:

WHISPERWOOD FARM
TOR & SAMANTHA NELSON

Silhouettes of mares and foals decorated the top two corners of the sign. Below, a cross-country horse and rider were flanked by a dressage horse and a show jumper.

"Isn't it great Samantha's back?" Christina said.

Kevin grinned. "Dad's so happy, he doesn't even

mind that she and Tor are going to be concentrating on three-day eventing and show jumping instead of racing."

"I don't blame her for not wanting to work around racehorses," Dylan said seriously. "Don't forget, her mother died in a racing accident."

Kevin nodded gravely. "But that's not the only reason they've chosen sport horses. Tor was always into show jumping, and then when they worked in Ireland, Samantha found out how amazing eventing can be. She won a bunch of big three-day events with this stallion before he was retired to stud."

As they approached the old-fashioned whitewashed barn with its huge hayloft, a slim woman in jeans and a blue work shirt came out of the barn.

"Hey, Sam. Did he come?" Kevin stood in his stirrups as he called to his half-sister.

Samantha shaded her eyes and waved. As they got closer, Christina admired the tangled mass of long red hair that spilled out from under Samantha's faded blue bandanna. Even though Samantha was only six years younger than Christina's mother, she seemed more like a kid than a woman in her late twenties.

"He's here," Samantha said, her freckle-faced grin amazingly like Kevin's. "I'm surprised to see you out of bed so early on a Saturday morning."

"Are you kidding?" Christina said. "Kevin's been planning this all week."

"You must be Dylan." Samantha put one hand on

7

Dakota's shoulder and stretched up to shake Dylan's hand with the other. "I'm Samantha."

"Nice to meet you," Dylan said, grinning.

Kevin's face turned red. "Sorry. I should have introduced you guys."

"No problem," Sam said, shrugging. "You don't have to be formal around here." She glanced at Christina and mouthed, *He's cute.*

Now it was Christina's turn to blush. She'd always insisted that Dylan was just a friend, but Samantha knew Christina liked Dylan a lot.

"I hear you're an event rider, too," Samantha continued. "Maybe you and Christina can come for a lesson sometime."

Dylan nodded. "That would be great."

"So, where is he?" Kevin said, looking around.

"Tor? Oh, he went to town."

Christina enjoyed hearing Samantha tease Kevin. She wished she had an older sister. Even though Kevin hadn't seen Samantha very often while she lived in Ireland, they were still really close.

"You know who I mean," Kevin said.

"Oh, is it Finn you're wanting?" Samantha said, slipping into a broad Irish brogue. "Well, stick your horse in an empty stall, and come and take a peek."

The thirty-stall barn was mostly empty, very different from the days when Tor's parents had operated a show hunter and jumper business there. Now that Tor and Samantha were back in the United States, and Mr.

Nelson had retired from horses and was living in Arizona with his new wife, Tor was opening up the family farm again. He and Samantha were advertising for boarders, but it would be a while before all the stalls were full.

Christina led Sterling into the first empty stall. She loosened the mare's girth a hole and ran the stirrup irons up the leathers, tucking them in place so that they wouldn't bang into Sterling's sides. Then Christina flipped the reins back over the mare's head, patting her on the neck before slipping the buckled end through one of the stirrup irons so the reins couldn't get stepped on and broken.

"Don't you dare roll with your saddle on," Christina warned as she slid the heavy stall door on its casters until it was closed. "I won't be too long." When she peeked back, Sterling was exploring the stall with her nose.

"Nice place," Dylan commented, as they walked up the aisle with Kevin. Christina's long-legged stride matched his perfectly.

"By the time Sam and Tor get finished with it, I bet it will be the best event barn in Kentucky." Christina gave a little skip, and Dylan grinned at her. She knew he shared her dream of being an international-level event rider someday.

"And show jumping," Kevin reminded them. "That's Tor's specialty."

They turned left down an aisle that led to a smaller,

connecting barn, and followed Samantha's voice to a corner stall. Peering through the aluminum bars that formed the top four feet of the stall, Christina could see Samantha standing at the shoulder of a deep brown horse with golden dapples on his flanks and hindquarters.

"Meet Finn McCoul," Samantha said, pride evident in her voice.

"Awesome," Dylan exclaimed.

"Wow," Kevin murmured.

Christina just stared. The Irish Thoroughbred was massive, with big-boned legs and a head that was a third again as large as Sterling's. He shared the thin skin and intelligent eyes of an American Thoroughbred, but that was where the resemblance ended. Compared to Finn, the racehorses Christina had grown up with looked like skinny teenagers.

"I was just going to let him loose in the indoor arena to stretch his legs." Samantha tilted her head at them. "Will you get the door for me, Kev?"

"I'd like to see that guy go cross-country," Dylan said to Christina as they followed Samantha and Finn down the aisle to the indoor arena. "I bet he can practically walk over the fences."

Christina knew what he meant. At seventeen and a half hands, Finn's back was a good hand—four inches— higher than Samantha's head. She wondered what it would be like to ride him.

When Samantha unsnapped the lead line from his

halter, Finn stood for a few seconds as though he were posing for a picture. The star on his forehead was the only bit of white on his body. The rest was varying shades of gold-kissed brown that darkened to black on his legs, mane, and tail.

Sterling's whinny woke him up. The stallion went from a standstill to an elevated trot, tail lifted, his nose swinging back and forth as he sniffed the air curiously.

"He's beautiful," Christina breathed, watching the stallion's every move. "I bet you won't have any problem convincing people to bring their mares for breeding."

Samantha crossed her fingers. "That's the plan," she said. "Of course, until the breeding season starts in February, things are going to be tight around here. I'm going to be exercising some horses for your mom and dad until we get on our feet."

Christina nodded. Exercising the young racehorses paid well. It was also good part-time work because the horses were usually finished by eight o'clock in the morning.

They hung around until Samantha's first lesson of the day showed up. On the way back to the horses, Christina paused at the framed photographs hanging outside the tack room. One of them showed a horse and rider just as they cleared a pile of logs and were dropping into the pool below. The photographer had caught a wave of water as it flew up from the horse's front legs.

"Wow. Some splash."

Dylan looked over her shoulder. "That's Finn, isn't it?"

"And Sam," Kevin said, crowding beside them. "It's the water jump at the Badminton Horse Trials in England. There were six falls at that fence alone."

Christina laughed. "You sure know a lot for someone who doesn't event."

"Yeah, well," Kevin said, shrugging, "I read about it in *The Chronicle of the Horse*, since Samantha was competing."

Christina lingered over the photographs of Samantha riding dressage in a top hat and a coat with tails and Tor sailing over brightly painted jumps at least five feet high. But it was the cross-country pictures with Samantha and Finn flying over giants' tables and Normandy banks that made Christina's heart soar.

Someday she was going to ride like that.

Thursday afternoon after school, Christina twitched with impatience as her riding instructor, Mona Gardener, put the last jump pole in the cups and brushed the sand off her hands. Mona checked the distance between the four fences by walking them off herself—four of her long strides to one horse stride—then turned to face Christina, Dylan, and Katie Garrity, Christina's good friend.

"The spacing is a little tight before the oxer, but I

want you to let your horses figure it out for themselves," Mona said. She stood with her legs apart, knees bent as though she were sitting on a horse. Christina could see the outline of leg muscles through Mona's fawn-colored breeches as she demonstrated the position she wanted them to use. "Establish a good forward trot to the first fence, sit tight, and let the horses do the rest."

Christina glanced at Dylan and Katie. It was the same routine as always. She knew that schooling through a grid—a row of closely spaced jumps—was good for the horses, but sometimes Christina wondered if they'd ever get to the big fences. She'd never say it to Mona, but it was getting to be kind of boring for her.

"Okay, Chris. You first." Mona's gray eyes zeroed in on Christina as if she were reading her mind. "If everyone works hard on gymnastics, I'll set up a course next."

Sterling danced sideways when Christina gathered the reins. "None of that," Christina softly reprimanded. She closed her legs on the mare's sides and pressed her forward.

"Her back is too tight," Mona called. "She's going up and down instead of moving forward. Canter her in a circle until she's relaxed and supple."

Christina nodded, steering Sterling onto a twenty-meter circle around a panel jump. She rotated her inside hand—the hand closest to the center of the circle—as though she were turning a key in a lock, while at the same time placing her inside leg on the girth and her outside leg behind the girth to ask for a bend. Sterling softened her jaw and turned her head inward far enough so Christina could see her dark, shining eye.

"Good. Now supple her the other way."

Christina changed the bend so that Sterling's head was turned to the outside and they were countercantering. The mare grunted. "I know it's hard," Christina said, moving her outside rein up Sterling's neck for a quick rub. "You're a good girl."

As the tension left Sterling's back, the mare's stride got longer.

"Excellent," Mona said. "Now keep her just like that. Pretend this is dressage over fences."

Christina guided Sterling down the long side of the arena, careful to keep her mare's spine following the bend of the track. When Sterling saw the grid, she raised her head slightly, but her rhythm didn't falter. "Easy," Christina murmured as they approached the first fence.

Sterling's shoulders lifted and effortlessly popped over the two-and-a-half-foot vertical. As soon as they landed, they were faced with the second obstacle, a scant nine feet away. Sterling had to rock back on her haunches before sailing over the bounce.

"Good," Christina said, pressing the mare on with her calves toward the in-and-out. This time Sterling had room to take one canter stride before standing back and jumping the yellow-and-white poles with room to spare.

Christina laughed as she groped for her stirrup, which had slipped off her foot during the generous jump.

The last fence was an oxer, a three-foot spread with two top poles of equal height. Christina was tempted to ask Sterling to take two long canter strides, then jump the fence big, but she remembered Mona's instructions.

"It's all yours," Christina said under her breath, keeping her hands and body quiet and her legs firm against Sterling's sides. The mare took two strides, then a short, quick third stride before popping over the fence in a jump that was anything but smooth.

I knew I should have done it in two strides, Christina thought as she started to pull Sterling up.

"Well done, Chris. Now do it again," Mona said, motioning her to circle around.

Well done? It didn't feel well done, Christina thought, shaking her head as they cantered around the ring and approached the gymnastics once more.

"This time, try closing your eyes before the last fence," Mona added.

Close my eyes? Why? But before Christina had a chance to ask, Sterling had jumped the first obstacle and was cantering on to the next. This time the mare adjusted her stride so that each fence was a perfect arc. When Sterling landed after the in-and-out, Mona shouted, "Now!"

Christina squeezed her eyes shut, and suddenly Sterling's movements felt magnified. She was aware of each stride, from the moment Sterling's hooves met the ground to when they paused, suspended in midair.

After the third stride, she felt Sterling rock back and soar though the air. By the time she opened her eyes, they were cantering smoothly away from the oxer. Christina patted Sterling's neck and then looked to Mona for direction.

"Go ahead and walk," Mona said, striding over to meet them. "That is exactly what I wanted to see happen on this exercise. You were piloting Sterling too much the first time, and you both made a mistake and got in too close to the oxer. Since your eyes were closed the second time, you didn't rush her into the takeoff. Instead, Sterling had to use her own judgment, and she applied what she learned from her experience the first time through."

Christina was confused. "Wouldn't it have been better if I had told her to take it in two strides?"

Mona shook her head. "Then she would have had to blast over the fence. That could be dangerous. If it were a big, preliminary-level fence, she might not have made it."

Mona turned to Dylan and Katie as she continued. "There will be times when you'll make mistakes riding into fences—especially over some of the trickier cross-country ones. If you've schooled your horses correctly, they'll be able to get you and themselves out of trouble. But they won't be able to do that if you've done all their thinking for them. That's why we do the gymnastics," she said, tapping her head. "It teaches them to think."

"But Sterling jumps regular fences better than the

grids," Christina protested. "How will she be ready to go up to training level if we don't practice over bigger jumps?"

Mona cocked her head toward Christina. "I know that you think Sterling's ready to do more. Maybe she is. But your first few eventing experiences are critical in forming a trust between the two of you. Remember what happened when you pushed her too fast last spring?"

Christina thought it was unfair to bring up the time when Sterling had gotten a little sour about jumping, especially since she had worked out of it. "But that was months ago, when Sterling was right off the track," she argued.

"Sterling's made a lot of progress," Mona said, brushing a hand through her short dark hair, "but she's still inexperienced. You don't want to overface her and ruin your chance of forming a partnership between the two of you." Mona gave Christina her end-of-discussion look.

Christina sighed as she stroked Sterling's sweaty neck. Overfacing was when horses were made to jump fences that were too difficult for them. But she wasn't doing that to Sterling. Christina didn't care if Mona was an expert horsewoman and her mother's best friend. This time the instructor was underestimating her. Couldn't she see that Christina and Sterling were partners already?

2

TWO DAYS LATER CHRISTINA LOOKED OUT THE WINDOW OF the old farmhouse that had been her home from the time she was born. "Samantha's here," she said, grabbing her windbreaker from the wooden peg in the alcove off the kitchen.

Melanie Graham, Christina's thirteen-year-old cousin, shoved the last part of her bagel into her mouth as she jumped up from the cluttered kitchen table. Even though her short blond hair was tousled from sleeping, she still managed to look good in a funky kind of way. Her baggy painter pants and man-sized button-down shirt over a tank top emphasized her petite frame, which sometimes made Christina feel like a basketball player beside her. Christina supposed it was growing up in New York City that gave Melanie her flair.

Not that Christina was a slouch herself. She was tall

and thin, and she had her own comfortable style. That day she was wearing a red rugby shirt, jeans, and brown leather zip-up paddock boots. She'd decided to let her hair hang loose for a change, now that the weather had finally turned cooler.

They were on their way to a horse auction with Samantha. Christina hoped they'd get back in time for her to take Sterling out for a long ride. *It would be a shame not to go out riding on a beautiful fall day like this*, she thought.

"Why is Samantha bringing a trailer?" Melanie asked as they ran down the driveway toward the Nelsons' rig, a dark blue pickup pulling a white four-horse trailer.

"So she doesn't have to make a trip back if she ends up buying some horses." Christina opened the passenger door of the truck. "Hi, Sam."

"Hey, guys. Hop in front." Samantha had left her bandanna at home, and her red hair was pulled back in a loose French twist.

Christina slid across the bench seat, straddling the gear knob so Samantha could shift. As she clicked the seatbelt into place Melanie asked, "Where's Tor?"

"He had lessons to teach, and some people are coming by to talk to him about training their horses." Samantha flashed them a grin before starting the engine. "So it's just us girls."

Melanie grabbed the auction flyer off the cluttered dashboard as they turned out of Whitebrook. "So, is

there going to be an auctioneer that nobody can understand?"

"You've got it." Samantha laughed. "Whatever you
do, don't scratch your nose or wave your hand during
the sale, or you might find you've bought a horse."

"I wish," Melanie said.

Melanie was from New York City, but she loved
horses, and the two didn't mix very well. Melanie's
father, Christina's Uncle Will, and his wife, Susan, had
allowed Melanie to come and live in Kentucky with
Christina's family. Ever since then, Melanie was getting
more and more serious about Thoroughbred racing.
Melanie's big hope was that someday she'd raise a
young Thoroughbred that she could train to be a champion racehorse, the way Ashleigh had done with a mare
named Wonder when she was about their age.

They arrived at the auction yard in time to walk
through the barns and look the horses over before the
bidding began. The stalls were tiny and old compared
to the ones at Whitebrook, but they were clean, and the
piney smell of fresh sawdust filled Christina's nose.

"Hello, cutie," Melanie said, stopping to rub the face
of a handsome bay who stood with his head over the
stall door. The horse pinned his ears back and retreated
to a dim corner. A square piece of paper with the number 32 pasted on his hindquarters stood out against his
reddish brown coat.

Melanie leaned on the door. "I guess he's not too
friendly after all."

"Look at his legs, poor thing," Christina said. The gelding's knees were swollen and misshapen. "I hate it when trainers push racehorses to the point where they break down. I'm glad Mom and Dad aren't like that."

Samantha came up behind them and shook her head when she looked into the stall. "He's not going to be good for anything but light trail riding, if he's lucky."

Christina knew what she meant. Horses that were lame sometimes ended up being bought by meat-packers. That was the worst part about auctions. Christina wished she could take home all the unwanted horses and turn them out in Whitebrook's pastures.

"Come on," Samantha said, steering Christina and Melanie away. "We're looking for horses I can reschool and sell as event or show prospects. Be on the lookout for nice mares, too, even if their legs or feet aren't in perfect shape. We can fix them up so they're comfortable. Remember, broodmares don't have to be a hundred percent sound."

They decided to split up. Christina and Melanie would check out the horses in that barn, while Samantha looked in the barn next door. "If you see something nice, come find me," Samantha said over her shoulder as she walked away.

"This is fun," Melanie said as they peeked over the stall doors, patting noses of all colors. "I've never been horse shopping before."

Christina paused at an empty stall, reading the card that was taped to the door. "This one sounds good," she said. "I wonder where she is."

Melanie read the card aloud. "'Foxglove: six-year-old bay English Thoroughbred mare out of Fancy Martha by Finnigan's Chase. Timber-raced in England.'" Melanie looked up. "I thought these horses were all from racetracks and farms around here."

"Most of them are, I think. I wonder what her story is." Christina took note of the number—27—and pressed on. "Let's remember to look out for her."

By the time they'd arrived at the end of the aisle, three horses had made their list: two bays and one dappled gray.

"You just like her because she reminds you of Sterling," Melanie said as they went to find Samantha.

"That scrawny thing?" Christina poked Melanie in the side. "Sterling is much prettier."

"Then why did you write down her number?"

"She's got a good frame with a long, sloping shoulder. With more weight and muscle, she'd be nice." Christina shaded her eyes against the golden autumn sunshine as they left the dim barn. Some of the sale horses were being led around a grassy paddock. She touched Melanie's arm. "Hold on, Mel. I want to look here for a second," she said, hoping to spot the English mare, number 27.

One small-boned bay with darting eyes showing rims of white was prancing nervously by her handler.

Christina was relieved to see number 19 pasted to the mare's hindquarters.

Across the way, a deep bay with a white star caught her eye. Her big head was nicely set on an equally large neck, and from her round barrel, she looked as though she'd been spending more time in a grassy field than on a racetrack.

"Can you see the number on that one?" Christina asked.

Melanie squinted. "Twenty-one, I think. Or maybe twenty-seven." She turned to Christina. "That horse doesn't look like any Thoroughbred I've ever seen."

"I bet she's the mare from England," Christina said, ducking through the white post-and-rail fence for a better look. "English Thoroughbreds have bigger bones than American ones."

At the mare's head was a tall, middle-aged man in a smooth leather coat who looked like he'd rather be anywhere else than at a horse auction. He was talking to a man and a boy about Christina and Melanie's age.

"My ex imported her last spring, planning to use her for fox hunting. But then she decided to run off and find herself, so I've been stuck with the stupid animal," the man holding the mare was saying as they approached.

Christina bristled at his harsh comment. It was obvious from the mare's beautiful, wide-set eyes that she was anything but stupid. Christina pulled Melanie back a few steps and whispered in her ear.

"This guy doesn't know anything about horses. If

that mare moves as nice as she looks, I bet Sam will snap her up."

"What if someone else wants her?" Melanie said, nodding toward the two people by the owner.

Christina glanced at the tall man with a well-worn flat hat covering most of his gray hair. Even though his back was turned to her, there was something familiar about him. Next to him, a lanky, dark-haired teenager smiled when he saw Christina looking at them.

"Come on," Christina said, her cheeks hot as she pulled at Melanie's sleeve. "Let's go get Samantha."

By the time they got back to the ring, the mare was gone. "She must be in her stall," Melanie said.

Samantha glanced at her watch. "Well, there's still time to take a peek before the bidding starts."

Samantha glanced into all the stalls as they worked their way back. "What do you think of this one?" she said, pausing by an angular deep brown horse with no white markings except for the number 8 pasted to his hindquarters.

Christina noted his clean legs and elegant head. "He's a little on the small side, but other than that, I guess he's nice."

Samantha nodded. "I'm not worried about size. He's only two, so he has a little growing left. Look at that short back and those strong hocks. I bet he'll make a good jumper."

Now that Samantha pointed out his nice conformation, Christina felt sheepish that she'd overlooked him before. "I guess I didn't pay enough attention."

"He's not the flashy kind of horse that catches your eye." Samantha put a check by number 8 in her program.

When they got to number 27 and Christina saw the English mare's large, inquisitive face and powerful body, which looked even bigger inside the stall, she felt a tingle of excitement. A glimpse of Sam's face confirmed her initial reaction. This was a mare worth considering.

"Now, don't get too excited," Samantha said as they climbed the cement stairs of the grandstand ten minutes later. "Chances are that mare will be out of my price range."

"Besides," Melanie said, sliding onto the long wooden bench beside Christina, "she might be a klutz with those big feet."

Samantha shook her head. "Don't let their size throw you off. If this mare timber-raced and still has legs that are clean and free from injury, she knows how to handle herself."

"Is timber racing the same as steeplechasing?" Melanie asked.

"Only in that the horses are racing over a course that has jumps," Samantha explained. "Steeplechase jumps have brush on top, so if a horse is going really fast, he can hang his feet a little over the fences without getting flipped."

Christina nodded. She'd watched the way steeple-chasers brushed through the long fences made of cut evergreen branches stuffed into wooden frames.

"Timber racing," Samantha continued, "is a race over fences that are built of solid timbers, like cross-country fences in eventing. It's pretty dangerous. If a horse hits one of those fences, he usually goes down."

Melanie swallowed. "I think I'll stick to flat racing."

"They're about to start," Christina said, nodding at the group of people who had been talking on the wide dirt track in front of the stands.

One of the men climbed onto the wooden platform that faced the grandstand. He picked up a microphone from the table.

"That's the auctioneer," Samantha said. Then she pointed to the man and woman who remained on the track. "And they're the assistants. They'll watch the stands for bids, then make sure that the auctioneer sees them." Samantha looked around the half-filled grandstand. "Not too many people here—" Her voice broke off, and she nudged Christina.

"Hey, isn't that Clay Townsend?"

Christina followed Sam's gaze to the far left side, down three rows of seats, where the gray-haired man she'd seen earlier was sitting. The cute boy who had grinned at her was on the other side of him. Now that Christina could see the gray-haired man's face, she recognized him instantly.

Clay Townsend was a big name in racing. He owned

Townsend Acres, the huge Thoroughbred farm where Christina's mother, Ashleigh, had lived as a teenager after a horse virus had closed down Edgardale, her family's old breeding farm. Many times Ashleigh had told Christina and Melanie how hard it had been for her parents to sell Edgardale and go to work for someone else. But Ashleigh always brightened when she added that if the virus hadn't sent her family to Townsend Acres, she never would've met Wonder, the Thoroughbred filly she had raised and trained to win the Kentucky Derby, with Ashleigh aboard.

"I wonder why Mr. Townsend is here," Samantha said, running her index finger along her jawline. "This is a pretty low-class sale by his standards. With the kind of money he has, the only auctions where I'd expect to see him are the ones where they serve champagne."

"He's that rich?" Melanie said, flipping up the collar of her shirt as she watched Mr. Townsend. "Too bad."

Samantha's finger stopped. "Why?"

"He was talking to the man who owns the big bay mare we like," Christina said, frowning. "And he seemed really interested." Christina's eyes were drawn back to the boy beside Mr. Townsend. He was waving his hands while he talked to the older man, and he seemed too self-assured to be one of the Townsend Acres grooms. She wondered who he was.

Christina didn't have time to worry about Clay Townsend and the boy once the auction started. When the bid for the first horse—a flashy bay gelding with a trot so long that his handler could hardly keep up with him—was hovering at a thousand dollars, Christina wished she had the money from her college savings account. A horse like that could be reschooled and easily sold for ten times that price.

"I looked at him in the barn. He has an old bowed tendon," Samantha whispered.

So much for getting rich quick, Christina thought, sitting on her hands. Even though the tendon was healed now, problems could flare up later, causing the horse to go lame.

Samantha bid on the thin dappled gray mare but stopped when the price climbed to three thousand. "Too steep for us."

She had better luck with number 8, the two-year-old brown gelding. When the auctioneer banged his gavel at Samantha's final bid, Christina grabbed Melanie's arm.

"She got him!" Melanie exclaimed.

This is so cool, Christina thought. *We'll actually be going back to Whisperwood with a new horse in the trailer.*

Samantha's enthusiasm was a little more restrained. "I hope he'll turn into something nice."

"He will," Christina said, trying to reassure her. "He has a nice eye." She had been around horses long enough to know that you could tell a lot about a horse's personality by his expression.

It got cold sitting in the grandstand, so after a while Christina and Melanie went to get hot chocolate for the three of them.

"You're just in time," Samantha whispered as they came back with steaming cups and honey-glazed doughnuts. "The English mare—Foxglove—is next."

Christina looked to see if Mr. Townsend was still in the stands. He was, and much to Christina's dismay, the boy with him was pointing to the gate at the far side of the auction gallery, where the mare was fussing with her handler. Christina bit her lip as the gate opened and Foxglove sailed in. The bay was teeming with energy as she pranced alongside her handler like a Grand Prix dressage horse performing a passage.

The auctioneer started her off at one thousand dollars. When Christina glanced at Mr. Townsend, she was relieved to see him sitting motionless as the bidding climbed to two thousand dollars. Maybe he wasn't interested after all.

Samantha waited until the bidding slowed before she waved her program. Twenty-two hundred, twenty-five hundred. As the numbers went up, Christina's stomach sank. She knew Samantha and Tor were on a limited budget.

Samantha and a man standing in front of the bleachers with one foot resting on the bottom rail of the low white fence were the only two in the contest. At one point the man took off his cowboy hat and ran his fingers around the brim before nodding to the auctioneer. Five thousand.

Christina waited for Samantha to raise.

"Who bid five thousand?" Melanie whispered.

"That guy on the rail." Christina glared at him as he put the cowboy hat back on his head.

"What the heck. It's only money," Samantha muttered, waving her program to raise the bid to $5,250.

"Six thousand." The voice came from the left. It was Mr. Townsend.

"Six thousand, six thousand," the auctioneer sang. "Do I hear sixty-five?"

The man with the cowboy hat shook his head when the auctioneer looked in his direction. Christina scanned the stands to see if anyone else would join the in bidding.

"Hurry," Melanie said, leaning across Christina to Samantha.

"I can't go any higher."

Christina could see the disappointment in Samantha's eyes. They both jumped when the auctioneer brought down his gavel.

"Sold to Mr. Townsend for six thousand dollars. You've bought yourself a nice mare, sir."

The dark-haired boy stood up and whooped, his fist punching the air. Mr. Townsend grabbed the hem of the boy's sweater and pulled him back into his seat.

Christina sighed. *That mare could have been the start of Sam and Tor's line of sport horses. Why did Mr. Townsend have to buy her, anyway? He has more nice horses than he needs as it is.*

"Well, I'm sorry we didn't get Foxglove," Samantha said after the auction was over and they were pushing through the crowds to get to the office. "But I'm happy with the horses we found."

Besides the brown two-year-old, Samantha had bought a big bay mare with a bone spur in her ankle that would keep her from being useful for anything but breeding. Still, selling one nice foal from the mare could pay back her purchase price, and with some luck she would have a lot of nice foals.

"There's that Townsend guy," Melanie said, lifting her chin toward the man in front of the cashier's window. Christina could see Mr. Townsend peeling bills from a silver clip and pushing them under the glass. She couldn't imagine carrying around that kind of money in cash.

Apparently the boy with him couldn't, either. "What did you do, rob a bank?" he said in a joking voice.

"He sounds English," Melanie whispered. "Don't you love his accent?"

"Shhh," Christina said, bumping Melanie with her shoulder. She liked the way the boy talked, too, but she didn't want him to know they were talking about him.

"If this horse can keep you from getting tossed out of another school, I'll consider it money well spent," Mr. Townsend said, resting his hand on the boy's shoulder.

The boy nodded. "It will, sir. And thank you."

"Well, don't just stand there," Mr. Townsend said, suddenly gruff. "Go and get your mare."

The boy spun around and took off, almost running

into Christina. His dark eyebrows shot up. "Dance?" he said with a grin as he held out his hands.

Was this guy crazy? As Christina looked up at him, his smoky gray eyes bore into hers. "Maybe some other time," she said, bumping into Melanie as she backed away.

The boy dropped his arms, but instead of moving on, he cocked his head, still smiling. "You don't remember me, do you?"

Christina couldn't help but smile back. The boy was as lanky and friendly as a puppy. "Should I?"

He squinted one eye shut as he thought about it. "No, I guess you shouldn't. The last time you saw me, I looked a bit more like this." He suddenly sank like a marionette whose strings had been cut, puffing his cheeks out like a fat clown.

"What is he doing?" Melanie said.

But Christina was too busy putting two and two together to answer. "Parker?" she said, amazed. "You're Parker Townsend?"

Parker straightened with a flourish and bowed. "At your service, madam," he said, sounding like a butler.

Christina laughed. "I thought you were away at school. I haven't seen you around the racetrack for years." She turned to Melanie. "Parker used to bet me candy bars on which horses would win. He usually beat me, too."

"You were gambling against a master," Parker said devilishly.

"Yeah, right," Christina said, facing him again. "The only reason you won so much was because you were a year older and could read the odds." She laughed, remembering how mad she used to get when she lost. "You sure have changed."

"You mean I'm not short and pudgy anymore?" Parker demanded.

Christina's cheeks got hot. "No," she said defensively. "I mean, people change in—what is it? Three years?"

"Four," Parker said. "I was ten when my mother and father decided to ship me off to London."

Then Christina remembered his parents, Brad and Lavinia Townsend. Once Christina had knocked a glass of milk over at a racing banquet and Lavinia had said, loud enough for everyone else at the table to hear, that children should be left at home with a baby-sitter until they were old enough to behave. Parker's father was almost as bad. Brad Townsend was one of those trainers who looked as though he'd never gotten his hands dirty. He was one of Ashleigh's least favorite people in the racing world.

Something sharp pressed into Christina's side. "Hey," she said, moving away from what turned out to be Melanie's elbow. Her cousin cleared her throat and lifted her chin toward Parker.

"Oh, sorry. This is my cousin, Melanie," Christina said, finally catching on.

When Parker nodded and said hello, Christina

noticed that Melanie's head didn't even come up to his shoulder.

Melanie shook her hair out of her eyes as she smiled up at Parker. "So, is that horse going to be yours?"

"Righto," Parker said, his eyes lighting up. "My grandfather bought her for me. Saying that, I'd better go and fetch her." He stuck out his hand, and Christina took it without even thinking. His skin was warm.

"Well, it's good to see you again," he said, giving her hand a firm shake. He shook Melanie's hand, too. "Hope to see you again soon."

Christina smiled as she watched him trot off, his head sticking above most of the crowd as he weaved his way to the barn.

"Well, he's sure different," Melanie said, her eyes open wide.

"Yeah, he is," Christina agreed, still feeling Parker's strong grip. "Interesting."

"More interesting than Dylan?" Melanie teased.

"No." Christina said. But she wasn't really sure. There was something about Parker that was different from the boys she knew. Maybe it was the way he was so all-out happy about his new horse—more like a little kid instead of a teenager acting cool. Or maybe it was the way his smoky gray eyes looked down into hers.

On the way home in the truck, Christina and Melanie filled Samantha in about Parker being Mr. Townsend's grandson.

"His grandfather said something about him getting thrown out of school," Christina said.

Samantha chuckled. "I would like to have seen his parents' faces when that happened. Brad and Lavinia Townsend are the biggest snobs I've ever known. And I've been in the horse business long enough to have met quite a few," she added. "I'm sure your mother has told you about some of the awful things Brad did when they were young."

"Like what?" Christina asked, peeling off a ragged fingernail with her teeth. She always liked hearing Samantha's version of Ashleigh's stories.

"Well," Samantha said, "if it had been up to Brad, Wonder never would have made it to the racetrack."

"But Wonder was a great racehorse," Melanie interrupted. "She won a lot of big races."

"In spite of Brad's efforts to ruin her. He never wanted Wonder to succeed, so he sabotaged her training whenever he could."

"Sabotaged? How?" Melanie asked.

Christina had heard this story before. "By scaring her with a whip when she was first being trained," she said before Samantha could answer. "Wonder is still afraid of whips."

"From what your mom told me, if Brad had had his way, Wonder would have ended up at a sale like this." Samantha shook her head. "I don't know why he's always felt so competitive with Ashleigh."

Samantha and Melanie talked the rest of the way

home about racing. Christina was still thinking about Parker as they whizzed past the orange-, yellow-, and red-leafed trees flanking the highway. Parker hadn't seemed snobby at all. She wondered how well he could ride.

3

"HOW'S THIS?" MELANIE ASKED THE NEXT DAY.

Christina finished swinging onto Sterling's back before she looked at her cousin. Melanie had jacked her stirrups up short like a jockey's and was crouched low over the brown and white pinto she was riding.

"If Trib gets silly and bucks, you've had it," Christina said. "You don't have enough leg around him to hang on." She was speaking from experience, having fallen off Trib—her outgrown large pony—more times than she'd care to admit.

Melanie sat back in the saddle again. "Well, I need to practice riding like this if I'm going to be a jockey."

Kevin came out of the barn leading Jasper. He looked handsome in his jeans and leather chaps. Christina saw Melanie sit up straighter in the saddle.

"You want to practice on the track before we go

out?" Kevin said as he tightened Jasper's girth. "There's only a week before the hunt club race."

"Sure," Melanie said, her smile broadening. "You don't mind, do you?" she added, turning to Christina.

Christina shrugged. "No. I'll just watch."

Actually, she wished she were practicing for the Bluegrass Hunt Cup Races next Saturday, too. It was an annual fund-raising event for the local animal shelter, and Christina had ridden Trib in the juniors' flat race the previous fall. As much as she wanted to take Sterling in the race this year, she couldn't. The last thing the mare needed was to be put in a situation where she was reminded of her track days—at least, that's what her mother and Mona both said. They were probably right. It had taken months of reschooling to teach Sterling to walk, trot, and canter without bolting.

Christina stretched forward to flick a deerfly off Sterling's ear. "If we could race, we'd show them, hey, girl?" she whispered.

"What do we wear for this race, anyway?" Melanie asked.

Kevin shrugged. "Hunt coats and breeches, I guess."

"Like you're dressed for fox hunting," Christina explained. "You'll be running in the big field behind the hunt club."

Melanie's mouth froze open in pretend terror before she said, "Wait a minute. We don't have to race over those huge hedges, do we?"

"Not for the junior race. That's on the flat," Christina reassured her. Melanie didn't mind jumping in a ring, but riding over hilly fences wasn't her favorite thing.

"Too bad you're not going to ride in the point-to-point race with Dylan," Kevin said as they walked toward Whitebrook's training oval. "It would be almost like eventing—or at least the cross-country phase of eventing."

"Except for all the other horses running beside Sterling, egging her on." Christina rolled her eyes. "Even *I* know that would be suicide with a hothead like Sterling."

After walking and trotting around the training oval with the others, Christina moved off the track when Kevin and Melanie were ready to race.

"On your marks," Christina shouted. "Get set . . . go!"

Trib and Jasper leaped forward in tandem, but with Jasper's longer stride, Kevin was able to pull away as they entered the turn. Melanie and Trib didn't give up, though. As the two horses swept down the far side, Christina could see Melanie aiming for the rail so that Trib wouldn't lose ground on the next turn. Her cousin was crouched low over Trib's shoulders, her hands kneading his neck with each stride. As the pinto pushed his nose out and began gaining on Jasper, Kevin glanced back. It was a bad move, because Jasper drifted to the outside, giving Trib a clear shot on the rail.

"Go, go," Christina shouted, not really certain whom she was rooting for. Sterling lifted her head, her body trembling in excitement as Jasper and Trib flew past them. Christina knew that if it hadn't been for the railing, Sterling would have joined in the chase for sure.

Trib's short, powerful legs carried him closer and closer to Jasper, and by the time they swept past the winning post, the two were shoulder to shoulder.

"I won!" Melanie sang out.

"No way! It was definitely a tie," Kevin shouted. The two of them were still laughing when they walked back to Christina.

"That was such a blast," Melanie said, standing in her stirrups and patting Trib's neck. Even though the pony was blowing hard, he still had a spring in his step.

Jasper, on the other hand, had turned a bright copper color from sweat. He wasn't nearly as fit as Trib. "I thought you had me when you sneaked up on the rail like that," Kevin said. "When did you learn how to do that?"

Melanie put on a mysterious voice. "Zere ees much you don't know about me."

"Come on, you guys," Christina said as Sterling danced around impatiently. "I need to work off some of her energy, too."

They decided to hack over to Whisperwood Farm to check out the new cross-country fences Samantha had told them they were building.

They trotted single file through the woods, with Sterling in the lead—the only way she'd trot quietly in the company of other horses. Christina admired the golden canopy of leaves overhead. "Don't you just love fall?" she said as they came out into a field and dropped back to a walk. The vivid blue sky was broken only by dots of black as crows lifted from their picnic of leftover dried corn to circle, cawing, above the horses.

Melanie halted so that she could pull off her sweatshirt. "I can't make up my mind what to wear to the hunt ball next week," she said, settling her helmet back on her head and redoing the chin strap. "One minute it's freezing, and then it's hot."

Christina gave a shiver of anticipation when she thought about the Junior Hunt Ball, a formal dance held the evening of the hunt club race. Ashleigh had told her stories of the fun she'd had going to the ball when she was a teenager, and Christina had been counting the years until she was old enough to go, too. "How about the dress you wore to your dad's wedding?" Christina suggested.

Melanie wrinkled her nose. "I don't know how that would fit in with the horsy set."

"If you want to look horsy, you could always borrow a set of Whitebrook's silks," Kevin said, referring to the blue-and-white jackets and helmet covers the Whitebrook jockeys wore for racing.

"Oh, be quiet." Melanie swung her sweatshirt at him before tying it around her waist.

"Everything I have looks too babyish," Christina said. "I tried on a couple of Mom's dresses, but they're too short on me." Dylan was taking her to the ball, so

Christina wanted to look especially good. Then she remembered Parker and his cute English accent. She wondered if he would ride his new mare in the hunt club race, or if he'd be going to the ball.

"What's the big deal?" Kevin said. "It's only a dance."

"Well, it's easy for boys. You just have to rent a tuxedo," Christina complained, feeling a little disloyal to Dylan as she pushed Parker out of her mind.

"Yeah. And we have to worry about stuff like our dresses riding up when we lift our arms for a slow dance. Anyway," Melanie added, "it's my first hunt ball, and I want to look good."

"You always look good," Kevin said, his cheeks turning red. "Come on. Let's get going," he added quickly, squeezing Jasper into a trot again.

Melanie grinned, wrinkling her nose at Christina before nudging Trib into a trot, too. It was no secret that Kevin liked Melanie, and she knew her cousin felt the same way about Kevin. Christina thought they would make a great couple.

Sterling jumped from a walk to a canter, not wanting to be left behind. Christina laughed as she felt Sterling's powerful muscles coiling beneath her. "Okay," she said, opening her fingers and allowing Sterling to surge forward. "But only a hand gallop."

Kevin and Melanie urged their horses on, but Sterling swept past them with ground-covering strides, and soon she was well out in front of them. Again Christina found herself wishing they could ride in the hunt races. With Sterling's speed, she was sure they could win.

They walked the last mile, so the horses were cool and their coats were dry by the time they returned to Whisperwood. Tor Nelson was replacing a line of fence when they got to the farm. His dark blond hair was flecked with sawdust when he put down his power saw and hoisted a sixteen-foot board off a set of sawhorses.

"Want some help?" Kevin asked, already swinging off Jasper.

"Sure. You can untack Jasper and stick him in a stall. Or put him in the field behind the barn and he can eat grass." Tor mopped his forehead with the hem of his T-shirt. "I can put you to work, too," he said, grinning at Christina and Melanie. "How are you at digging postholes?"

"Piece of cake," Melanie said, flexing a decidedly tiny arm muscle.

"I don't know about postholes, but I'm good at nailing up fence boards," Christina offered.

"That's okay," Tor said. "If you want, see if you can give Samantha a hand. She's had it with the mess inside the house. Before I came out this morning, she was threatening to box everything up and send it to Goodwill."

Christina nodded. She hadn't been inside the Civil War–era farmhouse for a few years, but she remembered it being a jumble of old riding tack, magazines, dog beds, and so much furniture that it was hard to move without bumping into something. Her mother said it hadn't been quite that bad before Tor's parents got divorced. But after Tor's mother left, the clutter had multiplied, since Tor and his father didn't pay much attention to housekeeping.

After all three horses were peacefully grazing side by side, Kevin went to help Tor, while Christina and Melanie climbed the steps to the wide front porch.

"Samantha?" Christina said, calling through the partially opened door. She could see into the dim central hallway, where stacks of *The Chronicle of the Horse* and *Practical Horseman* were piled against the risers of the long staircase. Boots and shoes spilled out of the corner by the front door. It looked just the way Christina remembered it

"In here."

As they followed Sam's voice, Melanie giggled at the mess. "I wish Dad and Susan could see this. They'd never yell at me about my room again."

Samantha was sitting on the kitchen floor surrounded by pots and pans. "This place is a dump," she exploded. "I can't stand it anymore."

Christina looked at the boxes piled on the large kitchen table and the papers and dishes covering the counters. There wasn't even anyplace to eat. "Well, put us to work."

A slow grin spread over Samantha's face. "You mean it?" Then, as if she was worried they would change their minds, she pointed to the sink. "Grab a bucket and sponge and help me wipe out these cabinets. The dirt is so thick, it's pointless to put dishes away."

Two grimy hours later, the table was clear and the three of them were sitting and drinking hot cocoa from some stoneware mugs with a sky-blue glaze on the inside that Melanie had unearthed and restored to a polished brilliance.

"I can't believe it," Samantha said, looking in amazement at how much they'd accomplished. Scouring powder and elbow grease had transformed the kitchen into a worn but homey place. Even though the sun came in through windows that were still cloudy with dirt, the old-fashioned red and white enameled sink and the newly scrubbed counters and cabinets looked tidy and pleasant. And the only things left on the black and white tiled floor were the five boxes of junk that Samantha had cleared out.

"You could have a huge yard sale when you finish," Christina said. "This stuff is weird enough for people to buy." She held up a contraption that Samantha thought might be a meat grinder.

"I'm too tired to think about a yard sale," Samantha said. "For now, let's just stick the boxes in the attic."

"Attic?" Melanie's eyebrows shot up. "Cool. I love poking around in attics."

They had to rest at the second floor, balancing their boxes on the banister, before trudging up the narrower attic staircase. As Samantha pushed open the door,

45

Christina could smell the dry, dusty-sweet scent of old wood. She sneezed.

"Wow," Melanie said, dropping her box and peeking out the window. "We're really high up."

Christina had to duck under a timber to make room for Samantha. "There's so much stuff," she said, looking around at trunks, suitcases, picture frames, dressing tables, headboards, and other assorted furniture. "Maybe you could have an auction instead."

"Five generations' worth of junk." Samantha let out a huge sigh. "I wouldn't know where to start."

Melanie wove her way to a large trunk with a rounded top. "This looks like a pirate's chest."

"Watch out for mice," Samantha and Christina said in unison as Melanie unhitched the leather straps.

Christina laughed when her cousin jumped back. "Just move things slowly, so the mice have time to escape," she told Melanie.

"They can have all the time they want," Melanie said, scooting back to the patch of sunlight. "I'm waiting right here."

But Christina was curious about the trunk, so she made her way over and lifted the latch. As the lid opened, a waft of cedar tickled her nose.

"Whoa. Look at this," she said, drawing out a white gauze gown. "Is it a wedding dress or something?"

Samantha took it from her and carried it to the window, taking care to drape the long skirt over her arm so it wouldn't get snagged on the rough wood flooring. "It

46

looks like a lawn dress from the Victorian era," she said. "There are albums downstairs full of photographs of ladies in white dresses playing croquet or sitting on porches." She held it up to Melanie. "Pretty."

Melanie hugged the fabric around her. "Hey! Maybe we can find something up here for the hunt ball."

"To wear?" Christina said.

"No, to eat," Melanie answered, rolling her eyes. "Of course to wear. Vintage clothes are the coolest way to go in New York. We can be original."

"I don't know," Christina started, but Samantha interrupted.

"You're welcome to look through this stuff. Between the suitcases and trunks, you'll probably have your pick of fashions from the whole twentieth century."

Melanie's brown eyes were sparkling. "Wow. There's enough here to start your own antique clothing shop. You could call it Samantha's Attic or something."

"In my spare time, right?" Samantha made a face. "No, thanks. I have more than enough horse stuff to keep me busy." She glanced at her watch. "Speaking of which, I'd better start cleaning stalls now."

"And we'd better get back," Christina said. "I told Mom we'd be home in time to help with chores."

"Can we try some of these on later?" Melanie asked, carefully folding the dress and laying it back in the trunk.

"Anytime," Samantha said. "It's little enough thanks for helping me with the kitchen."

"Let's not tell Kevin about the clothes," Melanie whispered as they walked out to find him.

"Why not?" Christina asked, enjoying the rush of cool, fresh late afternoon air against her cheeks.

"So it will be a surprise." Melanie wiggled her eyebrows. "Don't you want to surprise Dylan at the ball?"

Christina thought about the way Dylan's eyes had lit up when he saw her dressed up for the rock concert at the event camp they'd gone to during the summer. "Yeah, I guess so," Christina agreed. "It'll be fun."

As they made their way back to Whitebrook at a brisk trot, Sterling suddenly lifted her head and whinnied at something down the trail. Seconds later a horse and rider galloped into sight. Christina pulled Sterling up short, with Trib and Jasper close behind her.

"Hold up," the rider said, bringing his horse to an abrupt halt two strides in front of them. His mare snorted and tossed her large, elegant head. Sweat had darkened her bay coat to almost black, but Christina recognized her right away. It was Foxglove, the mare from the auction, with an unmistakable Parker Townsend on her back.

"Hi, Parker." Christina said, smiling.

"Hello, Christina." Parker's narrow face lit up as though seeing her had made his day. Christina felt a little uncomfortable under his direct gaze.

"Y-You remember Kevin McLean, don't you?" she said, stammering a little. "His father trains horses for us."

"Of course I do. Hello, Kevin. Say, you don't still have that old pony of yours, do you? I remember the time I tried to ride him and couldn't stay on to save my life."

Kevin grinned. "Well, it looks like you've learned a few things since then."

Christina had to agree. Parker's long, thin legs curved around Foxglove's saddle as though they were molded into place. From the way he quietly steadied the mare as she danced to one side, eager to be off again, Christina could see that being on a horse was second nature to him.

"So, do you like your new horse?" Melanie asked. Christina detected a note of envy in her cousin's voice. Melanie rode Trib and Pirate, a blind ex-racehorse that she used to pony the young racehorses on Whitebrook's training oval, but Uncle Will had never gotten Melanie a horse for her very own.

"Foxy's smashing," Parker said, bending to pat Foxglove's neck. The bay's ears went forward for a second before she resumed her restless movements. "But she doesn't like to keep still, so I'll push off. Would you like to get together for a ride someday?"

Christina admired Parker's light touch on the reins. "Sure. That would be fun."

"Cheerio, then," Parker said, waving, as Foxglove broke into a canter. He disappeared around the bend, but Christina could still hear Foxglove's hooves pounding away.

"If he keeps up that pace, his mare will be really fit." Christina nudged Sterling into a walk again.

"Or really lame," Melanie said. "Don't forget that Brad Townsend is his father."

Christina remembered the stories her mother had told her about how Brad had almost messed up Wonder's chances of winning the Kentucky Derby by over-racing her in the weeks leading up to it. But Parker didn't seem to act much like his father. "At least he's a good rider," Christina pointed out, "not one of those people who bounce in the saddle and saw on their horse's mouth."

Kevin's face was skeptical. "Except good riding is more than just knowing how to sit a horse."

Melanie pushed Trib closer to Sterling. "I think he likes you," she whispered to Christina.

"No, he doesn't," Christina said, feeling her face get warm. "He was just trying to be friendly."

Melanie made a face that said she didn't believe her.

"Anyway," Christina whispered back, "I like Dylan. Okay?"

"Okay," Melanie said, dropping back beside Kevin again.

"What were you two plotting?" Kevin asked, reaching out to tickle Melanie in the side.

"Nothing," she said with a giggle as she twisted away.

Christina only half listened to them goofing around. *Was* Parker acting as though he liked her? At first she'd thought it was just her imagination, but Melanie had noticed it, too. Christina chewed the inside of her cheek. Even though Dylan was sort of her unofficial boyfriend, there was no harm in being friendly to Parker, was there?

When Sterling tossed her head and skittered to the side of the trail, eager to be off, Christina thought about the lanky boy sitting on Foxy as though he were part of the saddle. She smiled to herself. She was looking forward to getting to know Parker better.

4

CHRISTINA THOUGHT THAT THE SATURDAY OF THE HUNT CUP Races and Junior Hunt Ball would never come. While she was listening to her classmates' country reports in geography class on Thursday, she doodled in the margin of her notebook: a horse flying over a fence, a traditional black hunt cap with an upside-down bow in the back, a horse's head that turned out too long and narrow. In math on Friday, she chewed on her thumbnail as she watched the steady rain running down the windows.

But in spite of the weatherman's threat of lingering showers, the sun woke Christina on Saturday morning. As soon as her brain was fully awake, she leaped out of bed. On her way to the bathroom, she stopped to wake up Melanie, but her cousin's bed was already empty.

"Where's Mel?" Christina asked as she tramped down the back staircase into the kitchen.

Her father turned from the kitchen counter. "In the barn already, braiding Trib."

Christina peeked around her dad to see what he was doing. "Deviled eggs for the picnic? Yum!"

Ashleigh came in the back door with a half a watermelon in her arms. "So, the sleepyhead is finally up," she said, playfully pushing Christina out of the way with her hip. "Will you cut this up for the fruit salad? There are blueberries and grapes in the fridge and cantaloupe and peaches on the windowsill."

By the time they picked up Katie and drove to the hunt club, the sun had dried the grass and warmed the air to a perfect temperature. Christina's mom and dad spread out the red and black checked blanket while Christina and Katie climbed into the bed of the truck and began setting up the picnic buffet on the opened tailgate.

"Doesn't it feel funny not to be riding?" Katie asked. She wasn't crazy about racing Seabreeze with other horses, so she had decided to sit on the sidelines with Christina this year.

Christina hooked her thumbs in the back pockets of her jeans as she scanned the horses and riders in the field. Melanie, Kevin, and Dylan were hacking over, but she didn't see them yet. "Yeah," she admitted. "But it's kind of nice to watch from the ground every once in a while."

Kevin's parents, Ian and Beth McLean, pulled in beside the Reeses' truck.

"Did you see Kevin and Melanie?" Christina asked.

"They're coming," Ian said, running his hand through his red hair. "We passed them on the road."

"Hi," Samantha said, waving out the window as Tor parked their truck on the other side of the Reeses'. "I didn't have time to cook, but we brought chips and soda."

"This is going to be the world's largest picnic," Ashleigh said as she spread still another blanket. Tor helped her anchor the corners in the breeze with six-packs of cold soda. Before long, everyone was lounging and eating as they waited for the races to begin.

Melanie and Kevin rode across the field toward them. They were an elegant pair in tan breeches, tall black boots, and navy blue hunt coats, their horses' manes and forelocks neatly braided.

"Save some food for us," Kevin complained.

"This potato salad is dee-lish," Katie teased, waving a fork.

Christina took pity on them and grabbed two of her father's deviled eggs. "Have you seen Dylan yet?" she asked as she passed the eggs up to them.

"He's hanging out with the other junior point-to-pointers," Melanie said, brushing bits of yolk off Trib's shoulder. "You know who else is racing with him?"

Christina finally spotted Dakota's shiny copper coat in the distance. She waved, but Dylan wasn't looking in her direction. "Who?"

"Parker Townsend."

Now Melanie had Christina's full attention. "You're kidding. He's only had Foxy a week."

"She is really wild today, too," Melanie continued. "Every time a horse trots or canters too close to her, she bucks."

"This I've got to see," Christina said, grabbing Katie. "Come on."

"Who's Parker?" Katie asked as they headed across the rolling field.

"Parker Townsend, son of the snootiest guy in racing, Brad Townsend." Christina was careful to sound nonchalant. "See that fancy group over there?" she added, turning and walking backward a few steps as she nodded toward the white canopy that was set up two picnics away from her family. Men in navy blue sport coats and woman in flowing dresses milled around a linen-covered table with platters and wineglasses. "Those are the Townsends. And that's their idea of a picnic."

Katie stopped. "Then why do you want to see this Parker guy?"

"I like his new horse," Christina said, only telling half the truth. "And I want to say hi to Dylan, too. Anyway, Parker's not like his father."

They spotted Dylan first.

"Hey," Dylan said when they got closer, his brown eyes crinkling. He looked especially handsome in his black hunt coat and tie as he sat on Dakota.

Christina grinned up at him. "Hey, yourself."

"Nice," Katie said, rubbing Dakota just below the

fat, crooked braids that marched down his neck.

"Are you making fun of his mane?" Dylan said, pretending to be hurt. "I can't help it if I'm all thumbs."

"It's fine," Christina said, trying to look sincere. "Are you guys ready to race?"

Dylan got serious. "I think so. I just don't know how he's going to be, jumping with all those other horses."

"You'll be careful, won't you, handsome?" Christina said, patting Dakota's shoulder.

A familiar voice came from behind. "Next she'll be telling us not to have any fun."

Christina jumped as she felt something warm tickling her neck. When she spun around, Foxglove was nuzzling her and Parker was laughing.

"Don't sneak up on me like that!" Christina said, surprised.

Parker pulled his long face into an apologetic grin. "I can't help it. Foxy does that to people," he said in a joking whisper. "I'm trying to break her of it. By the way," he added, holding out his hand to Dylan, "I'm Parker Townsend."

Dylan leaned out of the saddle to shake. "Dylan Becker."

Christina couldn't help but notice that Parker seemed more than just a year older than Dylan. Maybe it was because he'd lived away from home.

"And this is my friend Katie," Christina said, hoping that she hadn't been staring.

Parker smiled and said hi to Katie before turning

back to Dylan. "Do you know this course well?"

"Actually, this is the first time I've been in this point-to-point race, or any point-to-point," Dylan admitted.

"Really? Me too." Parker cleared his throat and straightened an invisible monocle. "What do you say we bring up the rear, old boy?"

Dylan swept off his hunt cap. "Lead the way, sir." His English accent was pretty lame next to Parker's.

"Oh, brother," Katie muttered. "What a couple of idiots."

The master of hounds—the man in the scarlet jacket who managed the dogs during a fox hunt—blew his hunting horn, calling the start of the race.

"We've got to get back. They're about to start," Christina said, spotting Kevin and Melanie with the group of riders and horses circling around the starting pole. "Good luck," she hollered, waving to them. "And be careful," she added, turning to Dylan. "You promised you'd dance with me tonight."

"Do the ladies wish me good fortune as well?" Parker said, still in his English-gentleman role.

Katie giggled. "Sure."

"Stop by the truck when you're finished," Christina called over her shoulder as she and Katie jogged off. "We've got tons of food."

Parker raised his hand. "It's a date."

Katie rolled her eyes as they headed toward the blankets. "He's really wacko. In a nice way, though," she amended.

"I know," Christina agreed. She'd never met anyone quite like Parker before.

They joined the others on the picnic blanket, eyes peeled to see their friends off. Instead of a starting gate for the races, a white line was limed across the grass.

"What if somebody jumps the gun and gets a head start?" Katie asked.

"They wouldn't dare," Ian replied. "Old Mrs. Wentworth-Buckley would come down on them like a pack of hounds."

Before he could say anything else, there was a squeal and a metallic crack from above. A voice filled the field.

"Good day." The words were loud, as though the woman was speaking with her mouth too close to the microphone. "Welcome to the forty-fourth annual Bluegrass Hunt Cup Races."

Ian cocked his head. "Speak of the devil," he said, grinning.

Mrs. Wentworth-Buckley was the great-granddaughter of the illustrious Hadley Wentworth, who had donated the grounds and chartered the Bluegrass Hunt Club. She was also the widow of Alastair Buckley, former master of hounds and founder of the Bluegrass Hunt Cup Races. As the woman made her speech, Christina watched the horses milling at the edges of the field. Melanie and Kevin were standing next to each other, and Christina could tell from the way Melanie kept checking her girth and stirrups that she was nervous. When Mrs. Wentworth-Buckley went off with another crackle, Melanie and Kevin picked up their reins and made their way to the starting line.

"Go, Mel! Go, Kevin!" Christina yelled. Katie stuck her fingers in her mouth and whistled.

They were too far away to hear the starter, who was standing on a platform, but when he dropped the red and white flag, the horses and riders were off at a gallop in a tight group.

It didn't take too long for the pack of twelve to spread out. An Appaloosa bucked and left its rider in the grass while it raced back to the starting line, whinnying to its friends. The rider ran after the horse, obviously unhurt but looking sheepish.

The course circled around the outside of the first three point-to-point fences. When the black horse in the lead passed the first hedge jump, Jasper was right on his tail. Trib and Melanie were farther back but holding their own in a group of three.

By the second hedge, the space between Kevin and the lead horse was increasing. Christina didn't know whether the black horse was accelerating or Jasper was just getting tired.

The third hedge was the turnaround point, where the course looped back to the starting line for the finish. The lead horse took the turn so fast, its legs started to slip out from under him. Christina didn't know how the girl managed to stay in the saddle, but her horse finally righted itself and galloped on. In the time the black horse took to regain his feet at the turn, Jasper was gaining again in second place, with Melanie and a gray horse a close third and fourth. Christina drew in her breath as Melanie slipped between the gray and the hedge, rocking back and circling the jump as if Trib were a Western barrel-racing pony.

"They're going to fall," Katie said, gasping.

But they didn't. Trib was the smallest horse in the group, but he was also the handiest. As they headed toward the finish, Trib's brown and white head inched past Jasper.

"Ride him, Mel!" Christina shouted. She leaned forward, her body rocking as if she were the one asking for speed.

But Melanie was already riding for all she was worth. She was stretched low against Trib's neck, her arms and legs like pistons pushing the pinto on. The black horse in the lead was tired. As Trib came up beside him the horse swished his tail and dropped back with his ears pinned, admitting defeat.

"She won!" Katie yelled, grabbing Christina and dancing a jig.

Everyone on the blanket was standing up and cheering.

"Well, what do you know," Ashleigh said to Mike. "I think we might have another jockey in the family."

When Melanie rode to the center of the field to accept her silver cup and blue rosette, Christina had never seen such a wide grin. After Kevin accepted his yellow ribbon for third place, he rode up beside Trib and leaned over, giving Melanie a quick kiss on the cheek.

"That is so sweet," Katie said. "Not many guys would do that after losing a race."

After all six ribbons were awarded, Kevin and Melanie brought the horses over to Ian's truck, where halters, buckets, and sponges were ready. By the time the junior point-to-point race was ready to begin, Jasper and Trib were cool and grazing by the truck while Kevin and Melanie juggled lead lines and roast beef sandwiches. Christina wished she could be riding with Dylan in the point-to-point instead of sitting there on the picnic blanket. She sighed as she turned her attention back to the field, where Dylan and Dakota were getting into position at the starting line.

Parker was having trouble getting Foxy into the lineup. Every time he brought her near the other horses, she half reared and pivoted away. Parker's long body stayed close to her neck as she stood on her hind legs. It almost looked as though he was whispering into her ear. Finally the big bay settled enough to stand at the end, about ten feet away from the rest of the horses. Parker nodded to the man on the platform, then sat calmly as if he were waiting for a bus.

"He sure is a gutsy rider, isn't he?" Katie whispered.

Christina nodded, full of admiration. She was a pretty gutsy rider herself most of the time, but it seemed that nothing could faze Parker.

The flag dropped and the group was off. Instead of surging forward with the rest of the horses, though, Foxy bucked and wheeled around. Parker kicked her forward, and for a second Christina thought the mare was going to jump up onto the starter's platform. At the last moment Parker steered to the left and pointed her at the first hedge.

The first hedge—all of the other horses were already over it, and Christina hadn't even been watching Dylan! She scanned the field, trying to pick Dakota out of the crowd. She finally spotted him at the outside edge of the course, cantering to the second fence with his head up and ears pricked forward. Christina was glad to see that Dylan had found a clear spot where he wouldn't have to worry about another horse drifting over in front of him. Dakota cantered easily up to the three-and-a-half-foot hedge and jumped it cleanly. Dylan must have closed his legs on the chestnut to ask for more speed, because Dakota lengthened his stride, surging past another horse as he landed, moving from sixth place into fifth.

Christina heard a collective gasp from the blanket behind her.

"Did you see that?" her father said.

Ashleigh answered, "That mare knows what she's doing."

Parker and Foxglove had jumped the first hedge and were galloping up the hill to the second. He wasn't doing anything to check the mare's speed before the jump. In fact, it looked as though he was pushing her on. Foxy hardly even broke stride as she sailed over the jump and galloped to the third.

Most of the field had slowed going down the hill to the fourth fence. Two riders had even pulled their horses back to a trot to rebalance them. Foxglove skimmed over the third fence and passed the two, her back rounded and her hind legs well under her as she charged down the hill. Parker came up so close to the next horse that Christina held her breath for fear they'd come down on the other side of the hedge in a tangle of legs. At the last second the rider pulled his horse's head to the right and drifted over, making more room for Parker.

"That was a dangerous stunt," Ian muttered.

"But it worked," Samantha pointed out to her father. "Being on the inside is going to improve his time."

Now Parker and Foxglove were bearing down on the two horses behind Dylan. Foxy lunged at one of the horses, her ears pinned back as she swept by. The horse weaved, almost hitting the horse on the other side of him. "Watch it!" Christina heard the rider yell.

"That's the way, kid!" The voice came from in front of the canopy, where Brad Townsend was punching the air as he cheered his son on.

From the sixth fence on, it was clear to Christina that Parker was going to win the race. When Dylan caught sight of Parker barreling toward him, he kept Dakota well to the outside. Parker was still riding to the inside edge of the hedges, jumping so close to the upright pole that Christina was surprised he didn't catch his boot. He didn't seem to care if he was jumping the fences uphill or down. Parker's tall body rocked forward and back, never seeming to interfere with the mare's natural balance.

Christina could feel the ground tremble under her feet as Foxy swept past them toward the finish. She could imagine just how fantastic Parker must be feeling to be riding such a powerful horse.

"All right!" she shouted, spinning around after Foxglove crossed the finish line at least ten seconds ahead of the second horse. "Weren't they wonderful?"

Katie, Beth, Ian, Tor, and her parents stared at her as if she'd lost her mind. Only Samantha seemed to understand.

"That's some mare," Sam agreed. "But it's a blessing they got around the course without breaking both their necks."

"What do you mean? Foxy jumped the hedges like they weren't even there."

Ashleigh put down her bowl of fruit. "Honey, if she had caught herself or stumbled going over the rough ground at that speed . . ." Her voice trailed off.

"But she didn't," Christina said. "Her weight was shifted back to her hindquarters just the way it was supposed to be. It was awesome."

"Are you talking about Foxy or Parker?" Melanie said as she pulled Trib's head from the grass and moved closer.

Christina flushed. "Foxy. Will you cut it out about—"
She broke off when she heard a voice behind her.

"Hi."

When Christina turned around, Dylan and Dakota were stopped in front of her. Dakota was still puffing a little, but his ears looked alert and happy from his run. Dylan's tie was crooked and his face was red and sweaty, but he looked happy, too.

"Hi," Christina said, her stomach sinking as she realized she had missed Dylan's finish. "You guys looked great!"

"I thought I was going to come off when Dakota stepped on his shoe," Dylan said.

Christina looked down and saw that Dakota's right front hoof was bare. "When did he do that?"

"Right as I was pulling him up after the race." Dylan looked puzzled. "Didn't you see him stumble?"

Fortunately, the PA system came back on just then to announce the results. Christina tried to make up for missing Dylan's finish by clapping extra hard when Dakota was called for sixth place. Parker tucked the silver cup he'd won under his arm and clapped, too.

A woman with a voluminous flowered dress called from the Townsend party, "Let's have a picture of the winning team. Bring that magnificent mare over here, young man."

"Lavinia, Brad, Clayton, you go over there . . . don't block the horse, though. She had a part in this, too."

Parker's mother, father, and grandfather looked as

though they were dressed for church. Christina giggled as Lavinia teetered across the grass in her heels, keeping her distance from Foxglove. *You'd think she'd never been near a horse before*, Christina thought.

"Push together more so I can see your faces. Lavinia, why don't you move between Parker and Brad?"

Lavinia tiptoed around Parker, glancing back as though she expected Foxy to grab her hat any second. The woman with the camera hollered, "Say cheese!" Parker put his arm around his mother and grinned.

When the woman finished taking the pictures, Lavinia moved away from Parker first. Christina didn't like the way she made a big deal about brushing off her blazer where his arm had rested.

"Darn, we should have brought a camera, too," Ashleigh said. "Especially since your parents couldn't make it, Dylan."

"Maybe we could get that lady in the dress to take one," Melanie said.

When Christina looked back, the woman with the camera had disappeared, and everyone else was heading back to the party table. Parker stood by himself in the grass, watching their retreat as he held Foxy's reins and the silver cup.

"Are there any sandwiches left?" Dylan asked as he loosened Dakota's girth. "I'm starved."

"I'll get you one," Christina said. She grabbed one for Parker, too. But when she turned around to take it to him, Parker and Foxglove were gone.

5

"WOW," DYLAN SAID AS CHRISTINA AND MELANIE MADE their entrance down the curving staircase at White-brook. In the two hours since they'd gotten home from the hunt races, they had undergone such a transformation that Christina felt as if she'd been zapped back in time.

She was wearing a long cranberry-colored velvet skirt that she'd found in Samantha's attic. Because the straight skirt had been fashioned in the days when no lady would show more than her ankles, it didn't even have a slit in the seam to make walking easier. Christina had to take small steps, lifting the hem when she ventured up or down the stairs.

Her blouse was made of delicate white cotton with a high, lace-trimmed collar and long puffy sleeves that Samantha called leg-o'-mutton. Melanie had insisted on fixing her hair, piling it into a loose bun. Christina put her hand up to brush away the strands that had escaped from Melanie's hairpins and were curling around her face.

"You guys look great," Kevin added, glancing at Christina before letting his eyes settle on Melanie. Her cousin looked like a flapper in the 1920s dress she'd found. The emerald green sleeveless shift fell to just above her knees. Every time Melanie moved, rows of black silk fringe shimmied with her. Even though Melanie's clunky platform sandals were not the kind of shoes girls had worn back then, Christina thought they completed the outfit perfectly.

Melanie rolled her eyes at Christina. "If we look so great, why are they calling us guys?"

"You know what I meant," Kevin said. He pulled a small box from behind his back and held it out to her.

"Here." Dylan handed Christina a box, too. Inside were pink rosebuds nestled on a bed of tiny white flowers and lace.

"A corsage! Thanks." Her hands shook a little as she lifted it out and held it up to her blouse.

"Thanks," Melanie echoed, holding a corsage, too. She brought the white flower to her nose. "Mmm. Smells good."

Kevin looked pleased with his choice. "Beth said her first corsage was a gardenia, so I decided to get you one, too."

"You both look so handsome in tuxedos," Ashleigh

said as she and Mike came in to greet the boys.

"Maybe we'd better change," Mike said, looking down at his flannel shirt and jeans and glancing at Ashleigh. "I don't know if they'll let us chaperone the ball in jeans."

"Chaperone? But Dad—" Christina broke off when she saw he was teasing. *Good thing,* she thought in relief. No way did she want her parents to be hanging around at her first junior hunt ball.

The hunt club was lit up like a Christmas tree when Dylan's father dropped them off.

"You really look pretty tonight," Dylan whispered to Christina as they followed the flagstone walkway, lit with candles glowing softly in oiled paper bags.

"Y-You do, too. I mean, y-you look really handsome," Christina stammered. She wished they could relax and talk normally instead of acting so stiff.

The ballroom of the old plantation house was longer than it was wide. In the golden light from the carriage lamps spaced on each side of the long, low windows, Christina could just make out the mural of an old-time hunt in the midst of a chase painted on the far wall.

"Want some punch?" Kevin asked.

Melanie shrugged, the fringe on her dress dancing in the dim light.

"I'll get us some, too," Dylan said, taking off as though he was glad to have something to do.

While they were waiting for Kevin and Dylan to

come back, Christina was relieved to see that there were lots of other girls in long dresses. Katie broke from a group and hurried over.

"Those outfits are *so* cool," she said. "I wish I had a vintage dress." Katie looked forlornly at her white dotted-Swiss peasant blouse and bandanna-fabric skirt whose foot-long ruffle dusted the floor.

"Are you kidding?" Christina said. "You look like someone from the Old West. It's perfect."

"Try this." Melanie shifted Katie's blouse so that it fell off one shoulder. "Now you look like a beautiful señorita—in a blond sort of way."

Katie giggled. "You think so?"

"Definitely!"

The DJ was playing music, but no one was dancing yet.

"I hope this isn't going to be one of those parties where the boys stay on one side of the room and the girls end up dancing with each other," Melanie said, looking at the guys crowding around the tables piled with food. Kevin and Dylan were talking with Katie's on-again, off-again boyfriend, Chad. They didn't seem in a hurry to get back.

Christina was about to say, "Me too," when she saw old Mrs. Wentworth-Buckley heading toward the door, one hand across her pearl necklace and a determined look in her eye.

"Young man." Mrs. Wentworth-Buckley's voice boomed over the music as she held out her hand like a policeman stopping traffic and stalked out to the entry hall.

"Let's head where the action is," Melanie said, pulling Christina and Katie out of the ballroom into the large foyer.

"Just where do you think you're going?" Even though Mrs. Wentworth-Buckley wasn't talking to them, Christina stopped. There was Parker, the center of the ruckus, standing at attention under the crystal chandelier. He smiled and winked at her before turning to the older woman.

"Up here," Melanie hissed, dragging Christina to the wide staircase where an arrow marked FILLIES pointed the way to the ladies' bathroom. Christina lifted her skirt to climb the stairs as far as the first landing, where she stopped with the others to watch the scene unfolding below. She giggled when she got her first full view of Parker.

From the waist up, Parker was decked out as though he were being presented to the queen. He wore a fitted black coat with sweeping tails over a canary-colored vest. A starched white ascot tied around his neck set off his long, aristocratic face, and a black silk stovepipe hat completed the picture of a self-assured gentleman.

But it was the bottom half of Parker that Mrs. Wentworth-Buckley was sputtering about. With a "Good evening, madam," Parker swept off his hat and bowed all the way to his denim-covered knees.

Christina tried hard not to laugh when she saw

Parker's huge, scuffed Nikes sticking out below his skinny, blue-jean-clad legs, but a snort escaped anyway. She clamped her hand over her mouth and pretended to cough instead. Fortunately, Mrs. Wentworth-Buckley was too intent on her prey to notice.

"Young man," she began again, "this ball is for *formal* attire."

Parker straightened with a woebegone face that reminded Christina of a basset hound. "I'm terribly sorry," he said, really laying on the English accent. "A recent growth spurt rendered my tuxedo pants useless, and I was hoping that the low lights would conceal my dilemma. Please forgive my faux pas. I will leave at once." When he reached into the silk hat and pulled out a nosegay of flowers, Mrs. Wentworth-Buckley's mouth dropped open.

"Thank you again for the delightful hunt races this afternoon," Parker said, presenting the bouquet with a flourish. "I had a smashing good time." As he turned to leave, he looked up and raised his eyebrows at Christina.

"Well, now," Mrs. Wentworth-Buckley said hesitantly. "I think that under those circumstances we can overlook your ensemble."

"Really?" The assured-gentleman look was gone as Parker grinned at Mrs. Wentworth-Buckley. "Ta. I mean, thanks!"

Melanie looked at Christina. "And my father accuses *me* of being manipulative."

"Ta?" Christina asked Parker later when a group of them had gone out on the porch to cool off after dancing.

Parker laughed. "It's slang for 'thank you' in England."

"Like *lorry* for 'truck'?" asked Chad.

"And *petrol* for 'gas,' *loo* for 'bathroom,'" Parker added. "Even though we're supposed to speak the same language, you'd be amazed at how often I was asking, 'What?' when I first went over."

Melanie hoisted herself onto the railing. "So why did you get thrown out of school?" she asked.

"Subtle. Real subtle, Mel," Christina whispered. But she didn't have to worry about Parker being embarrassed. He flopped into a wicker rocking chair and laughed.

"I borrowed a car," he said, as if that explained everything.

"They threw you out for that?" Dylan said. "English schools must be a lot stricter than the ones here."

"You drive?" Chad sounded impressed. "How old are you, anyway?"

Parker shook his head sadly. "Fourteen. That was one of the things the bobbies brought up."

"Bobbies?" Melanie looked at Parker as though he were speaking gibberish.

This time Dylan answered. "Police. You got in trouble with the cops?"

"Well, it seems that the car was reported stolen."

"Wait a minute," Katie said, pulling up a chair. "Why don't you just start at the beginning?"

Christina watched Parker's face as he told them about the teacher who took pity on him when he had nowhere to go on the weekends he didn't get invited home by one of the other boys. That teacher would have him to tea (supper, Parker translated) or take him to the pictures (movies). One time he even showed Parker how to drive his Mini-Cooper, and Parker spent several hours in bliss tooling around the school grounds.

"So you stole the car?" Dylan asked.

"Borrowed," Parker corrected. "I had to get to the racetrack."

"Racetrack?" Melanie hooked her arm around the post and leaned forward.

Parker turned to her. "My grandfather has several racehorses in England, and on school holidays I would stay at his trainer's stable."

Christina noticed a shadow slip over Parker's face, as though he was bothered by something.

"And . . . ?" Katie prompted when Parker just sat there, studying his shoes.

When Parker looked up to answer, the shadow was gone. "I hadn't been there in a while, so I just decided to go," he said with a shrug, a rakish grin lighting his face.

Christina looked at Parker, wondering if she'd imagined his moment of discomfort. He jumped up and moved around to the back of the chair, standing on the runners. "And then there was the time some mates and

I borrowed people's hoses—only they called them hosepipes—and fastened them together so we could lower ourselves down into one of those forty-foot-high water towers."

As he told them the story, Parker worked his face like a rubber mask, twisting it into the suspicious dorm monitor or stretching it with the glee of a drunken schoolboy. His eyes glowed as he described climbing out the second-story windows of their dorm, with only the ivy to hang on to. Christina could almost feel the energy pulsating from him.

He was a natural storyteller, too, that was for sure. When Christina glanced around at one point, everyone was spellbound. She wondered about his racetrack adventure, though. It seemed as though there was something he was leaving out.

Later that evening, Christina and Dylan had just started a slow dance when Parker came over and tapped Dylan on the shoulder.

"May I?" he asked. His gray eyes looked black in the dim light.

Christina smiled, then looked at Dylan to see if he minded. Dylan stepped back as if he wasn't sure what he was supposed to do.

"Thanks, mate," Parker said, putting one arm around Christina's waist. He took her hand and held it against his shoulder as he turned her away, his long legs taking bigger dance steps than Christina's vintage skirt would allow.

"Whoa," Christina said, falling against his chest as she lost her balance.

"Sorry," Parker said, steadying her with both hands around her waist. He didn't seem sorry at all.

Christina grinned back. "Okay, but take it easy. This skirt wasn't made for extended trots."

The way Parker threw back his head and laughed at her joke made Christina feel good. She gave her head a little shake to get the curly hairs away from her eyes before teasing him some more.

"So, when you weren't *borrowing* cars, how did you usually get to the racetrack in England?"

"Train," Parker said. "Hey, I heard there's a hunter pace at River Oaks Farm next weekend. Do you know anyone who needs a partner?"

Hunter paces were almost as much fun as the cross-country phase of events. Riders went out in pairs over a set course, riding at the pace they would go if they were out fox hunting with a group. The pair that came closest to the secret, optimal time was the winner.

"I need one." The words were out of Christina's mouth before she had a chance to really think about them. "Dylan wanted to do it with me, but he has to go to his cousin's wedding. And Melanie's riding with Kevin." She had been trying to talk Katie into skipping her gymnastics meet to ride in the hunter pace, but the prospect of riding with Parker sounded more exciting.

"We'll ride together, then," Parker said, squeezing her hand and letting it go just as the song ended. He leaned forward and whispered in her ear. "Tell Dylan he has the prettiest date at the ball."

Christina followed his nod to where Dylan was looking trapped by one of the women who was chaperoning. Poor Dylan, Christina thought as she hurried over to rescue him.

"Hi," she said, slipping up beside them.

"Hi." Dylan looked so glad to see her that Christina's stomach did a little flip.

I still like Dylan best, Christina thought, looking at his familiar, crooked smile. Before she could tell him that she was going to the hunter pace after all, the DJ put on an oldie and Melanie started rounding up everyone to do the twist. As Melanie began to wiggle and shimmy, hamming it up in her flapper dress, Christina laughed so hard her stomach hurt.

After she had collapsed into bed that night and was reliving the high points of the evening, Christina realized with a start that she couldn't get her dance with Parker out of her mind. She rolled onto her back and looked at the moon outside her window.

Is it bad to like two boys at the same time? she wondered. *Parker's exciting and funny, but Dylan is as comfortable to be with as Rags.* Christina jumped up and rooted around until she found her old stuffed dog under her desk and brought him back to bed with her.

"What do you think?" she whispered to her old confidante. "Am I a terrible person?" But Rags's eyes just shone in the light from the window.

Christina sighed and turned on her side, tucking Rags into his old spot under her chin. She rubbed his satin ribbon until she drifted into sleep.

6

DYLAN DIDN'T SOUND TOO HAPPY WHEN CHRISTINA TOLD him on the phone Sunday night about riding with Parker the next weekend.

"You don't want me to stay home from the hunter pace just because you're going to be out of town, do you?" Christina asked, wishing he would be more supportive.

"No," Dylan said, but he didn't sound very sure. When they finally hung up, Christina went into Melanie's room to complain. Her cousin was sitting on the rug, listening to a CD while she did her math homework.

"Boys," Christina said, pushing the clothes to the end of her cousin's bed so she could sit down. "Just because I'm going to the hunter pace with Parker, Dylan's acting like I don't like him or something."

When Melanie took the pencil out of her mouth, Christina could see the tooth dents in the yellow wood. "How do you want him to act when you're going out with another boy?"

"I'm not *going out* with him," Christina said. "We're just riding together."

Melanie lifted her eyebrows. "Isn't that how you and Dylan got together?"

Christina looked at her cousin a few seconds before bursting out laughing. "I guess it is," she admitted.

"I rest my case," Melanie said, bending over her books again.

Christina tried to pay extra attention to Dylan in school that week, and by Thursday things felt back to normal again.

"You're lucky to be getting out of school tomorrow," Christina said as she tried to cram one too many textbooks into her backpack. "You'll miss Mrs. Logan's math test."

"No, I won't," Dylan said. "I had to take it during study hall today. Besides, I'd rather take a test any day instead of driving to Ohio for a stupid wedding." He took the extra book out of her hand and carried it as he walked her to the bus.

"Poor Dylan, having to dance with those twins," Christina teased. Dylan had let it slip that the bride had fourteen-year-old twin sisters who were going to be junior bridesmaids. She hoped they weren't too pretty.

"Yeah, while you get to ride in the hunter pace," Dylan said glumly. He didn't mention Parker.

"I promise not to have too good a time if you'll promise, too," Christina said.

Dylan grinned at her. "Deal."

Saturday morning was blustery and gray. Sterling scooted forward as a gust of wind whooshed under her tail.

"Cut that out," Christina said as Sterling bucked, pulling the reins out of her hands. "I know it's cold, but that's no reason to forget your manners." She squeezed the mare into a trot, schooling her in figure eights and three loop serpentines in the large open field as they warmed up for the hunter pace.

"Hello," Parker said, bringing Foxy alongside Sterling when Christina had come back to a walk.

"Hi." Christina noted with envy Parker's heavy Irish knit sweater under his safety vest. The wind was finding its way through her fleece pullover. "I was beginning to think you'd overslept or something. We're signed up to ride in fifteen minutes."

"It took longer than I thought to hack over." Parker's nose was red from the wind, but his eyes were sparkling. "Nice mare you've got."

"Thanks." Christina ran her hand down Sterling's warm, silky neck. "She's pretty great, all right."

"So why are you schooling? Isn't this supposed to be fun?"

"Self-preservation," Christina admitted. "If I don't get Sterling focused, she'll pull my arms out over the fences. Won't you, girl?"

As if in answer, Sterling brought her head around and blinked at Christina with a large brown eye. The mare's breath came out in warm, puffy clouds as Christina reached forward and ran the back of her fingers lightly along Sterling's velvety soft muzzle.

"Well, that's because you're not challenging her enough. Give her some bigger fences to concentrate on and I'll bet she'll slow down."

"You think so?" Christina said.

"Sure. That's what I've found out about Foxglove." Parker let Foxy and Sterling sniff each other's noses. Christina tensed a little, half expecting one of them to squeal or kick. But nothing happened.

"I guess they like each other," she said, squeezing Sterling into a walk.

Foxy walked, too. With their heads up and ears pricked eagerly forward, they looked as though they were ready for anything.

"Hi, Parker," Melanie said, riding up on Trib. "Brrr," she added to Christina. "Where's that hot cider you promised?"

"At the mandatory rest stop halfway through the course," Christina said.

Melanie shivered. "But I'll be a Popsicle by then."

"Not if we get moving," Kevin said, sneaking up behind her on Jasper. He leaned over and tapped her on the back. "Tag. You're it," he said, and then cantered away.

"Oh, yeah?" Melanie pulled Trib's head around and took off after him. "Don't forget who won the race last week!"

"Team three, you're on deck," a woman with a clipboard and mittens called.

"Righto," Parker said as they headed for the starting box. "This is the plan. They don't care which jumps we take, as long as we stick to the basic route, right?"

Christina nodded. Just like in a regular hunt, riders had the choice of jumping any part of the fences or riding around them. And River Oaks Farm had elementary- through preliminary-level cross-country fences.

"And you'd like to see what your mare can really do, right?"

"Yes," Christina said hesitantly, beginning to catch his drift.

Parker and Christina headed into the eight-by-eight-foot box that was fenced on three sides. They turned their horses and waited for the starter to begin the ten-second countdown. At other events, Christina had to keep Sterling facing backwards in the starting box, to keep her from bolting before the starter had finished the countdown. This time, Sterling was distracted by Foxy's presence in the box, and was hardly even fidgeting.

"Ten . . ."

Parker grinned and leaned over. "Follow the leader?"

Christina looked at the first fence. She had jumped the lowest part of it during the last event she'd ridden. The middle section was about three feet high, with gravel and a pole placed four feet in front of it for depth. The highest section to the right was about half a foot taller, but instead of gravel, it had a four-foot ditch.

"Sterling isn't ready for the ditch yet," Christina said, just as the starter called, "Go!" But Parker didn't seem to have heard.

"Tally ho!" He closed his legs on Foxy, and they shot out of the box at a gallop.

Sterling rocked back on her haunches and bolted after them as though it were a race. "Oh, no you don't," Christina said, sitting deep in the saddle and pressing her legs against Sterling's sides. At the same time, she opened and closed her fingers on the reins as though she were squeezing water out of a sponge. If Sterling didn't respond to these half-halts, the mare might jump too flat and hit the fence.

Parker jumped the middle portion of the brush, much to Christina's relief. She aimed Sterling toward the same spot, still asking the mare to shift her weight back into a rounder, more controllable canter. But Sterling was more concerned about Foxy disappearing across the field than the jump. She lifted her head and whinnied, ignoring the looming fence.

"Sterling," Christina pleaded, sinking even further

into the saddle as she fought to get the mare's attention. Three strides away from takeoff, Sterling caught sight of the pole and gravel and faltered. This was just the moment Christina needed. She closed her legs on Sterling's sides and pushed her on.

Now Sterling was all business. She took two measured strides, then rocked back and sailed over the hedge in a graceful arc. Seconds later, her front feet hit the ground and they were off again, galloping across the grass.

Only this time it was different. Sterling's neck and shoulders were up and her body felt like a huge spring, ready to shoot in whatever direction Christina pointed. They were going fast, but they were going as a team, not fighting each other. As Sterling blew out rhythmic puffs that matched the thunder of her hooves, Christina couldn't stop grinning. This was riding!

Christina and Sterling jumped a stone wall and a wagon built of hay bales and old wagon wheels. As they soared over each obstacle, Sterling landed with her head up and ears forward, eagerly looking around for the next fence.

They finally caught up to Parker on the logging road that wound through telephone-pole-sized pine trees. He'd pulled back to a walk and was turned in the saddle, waiting for her.

"How's she doing?" Parker said with a mischievous twinkle in his eye.

"Great," Christina said. "I thought we were goners

at first, but you should have seen the way she took those fences. I think you're right—the higher jumps are making her think more about what she's doing."

They ended up jumping everything they went by: white coops, log structures, picket fences, and jumps made of tires, picnic tables, and wooden drums. Parker even helped her get Sterling up her first Irish bank, which was like a giant sandbox packed tightly with dirt. Sterling trotted the two-foot side first, leaping up after Foxy and cantering two strides across the top before heading down the ramp on the other side. Then Christina tried the more difficult approach, where Sterling had to jump up the three-foot side, take two strides across the top of the bank, then leap off a three-foot drop to the ground below.

"This is such a blast," Christina said, rocking forward to put her arms around Sterling's neck as they walked to cool off before the halfway checkpoint. The mare's silver dapples had darkened to pewter from sweat. Her shiny black mane tickled Christina's cheek as she drank in the sweet smell of shampoo, leather, and horse.

She could tell that Sterling loved it, too. The edgy nervousness had gone out of her stride, and she was walking along beside Foxy as though she hadn't a worry in the world.

Parker seemed more relaxed, too. He had a faraway look as one hand rested on his breeches, his seat automatically following Foxy's stride. When he turned to

Christina, his smoky gray eyes were soft. "Sometimes I think that the only time I'm completely happy is when I'm riding."

Christina nodded. "It is the greatest." But part of her wondered what he meant.

After handing Christina and Parker steaming cups of hot cider at the checkpoint, the two helpers hopped back into their four-by-four, out of the wind. Christina dropped her stirrups, wiggling her toes in her boots to warm up as she let her feet dangle.

"So how come you're into eventing instead of racing?" Parker asked.

Christina shrugged. "Racing's okay, but jumping is so much more exciting. And it's not as if I could ever be a jockey anyway," she added, stretching out her long legs. "I'm so tall, I'd have to be a skeleton to make the weight."

"Tell me about it," Parker said. "I was all set to be a jockey until I grew six inches last year. And I'm still growing," he added with a frown. "I can't even be a jump jockey now."

Christina felt bad for Parker. "How about eventing?" she said, trying to cheer him up. "Once you work your way to preliminary level and can go cross-country without any jumping penalties, you can ride in three-day events. And those have steeplechasing as part of the endurance phase."

Parker raised his eyebrows. "You sound like an expert. What level are you doing with Sterling?"

"Only novice so far," Christina said. "But that's because Sterling's new at eventing. I know she has a lot of talent, though. In a couple of years, I'm planning to try out for the Young Riders team with her so we can compete at the biggest events in the country. A lot of Young Riders end up riding on the United States Combined Training Team when they get older. That's what I'm aiming for," she finished, suddenly worrying that she sounded like a show-off.

If Parker thought her dream was silly, he didn't give any sign of it. "How high do novice horses jump?"

"Two feet eleven inches, but brush fences can be four inches taller," Christina said, reciting the rule book. "And jumps can be four feet, seven inches wide at the bottom for cross-country, and just under five feet wide for show jumping."

Parker looked surprised. "Why are you doing novice? Sterling's jumping higher than that today."

"Yeah, I know," Christina said, sighing.

Parker raised his eyebrows. "You're not scared to move up, are you?"

"No!" His question annoyed her. Would she have kept up with Foxy in the hunter pace if she were scared? "My instructor thinks Sterling and I need more experience before we go to training level."

Parker just looked at her.

The four-by-four's door opened. "You can head out now," the girl said, waving before she disappeared back inside.

"After you," Parker said with a sweep of his arm.

As Christina gathered her reins and pressed Sterling into a walk, she wondered if Parker thought she was chicken. Sterling tossed her head and jigged forward, eagerly looking for the next jump. "We'll show him, won't we, girl?" Christina whispered. She stretched her heels down and locked her calves, tipping out of the saddle into a two-point position. "Let's go."

They pretended they were riders from an old English fox-hunting painting as they rode the last half of the course, laughing and dodging each other as they leaped across the fences. Finally they arrived at the finish, tired but elated. When Kevin and Melanie cantered into the finish twenty minutes later, Christina's cheeks were still warm.

"Why don't you ride back to Whitebrook with us?" Christina suggested to Parker. "We can stick Foxy in an extra stall, and Mom will drive us back for the awards and potluck dinner."

Parker's face lit up. "That would be fab. But I don't have anything to bring."

"Just bring yourself," Christina said, leaning back to stroke Sterling's hindquarters. "Melanie and I made enough brownies to feed an army."

When Ashleigh dropped them off at the potluck, the living room of the farmhouse was steamy with food and riders. Christina filled a paper plate with macaroni and cheese, chili, a slice of quiche, a huge slice of homemade bread, and Waldorf salad with raisins, nuts, and miniature marshmallows mixed in with the apples. She glanced at the table where her brownies were surrounded by cookies, carrot cake, fudge, and more brownies, but decided she'd better not try to fit anything else on her plate.

"Over here," Melanie called, patting the floor in front of the stone hearth. Christina was amazed to see that her cousin's plate was even fuller than her own.

It didn't take long for Parker to become the center of attention, though most of the other riders were adults. He joked about the time he'd borrowed a big workhorse and rode it in a ladies' sidesaddle class at a fancy show in England. His friend had helped him rig up a ladies' riding habit, complete with balloons tucked inside his shirt for authenticity, and they had to tie two girths together to go around the horse's barrel. Coming into the ring after the class had started, Parker had cantered once around, almost falling out of the sidesaddle. "Those women were jolly good riders to make it look so easy," he said.

Christina laughed with the rest, imagining the indignation of the stuffy ladies in their riding finery.

It wasn't until Christina looked at the last cookie on her plate and felt slightly sick to her stomach that Mr. Little, the host of the hunter pace, began to hand out awards. Melanie was pink with pleasure when she and Kevin came in third. "Wait until I tell Dad and Susan," she whispered when she came back with the gold ribbon.

Christina wasn't too surprised to find out that she and Parker had come in last since their time was too fast. It was kind of fun getting the Most Likely to Get in Trouble for Passing the Field Master award.

Parker leaned over and whispered in her ear. "Fox hunting is for old geezers, anyway," he said. "Eventing is where the real action is. Right?"

Christina nodded, remembering how good it had felt with Sterling sailing over the higher fences that morning. Parker was right. Sterling was ready for more speed and harder jumps.

But could Christina convince Mona of that?

7

"LET'S ASK MONA IF SHE'LL RAISE THE JUMPS," CHRISTINA said to Katie as they watched Dylan and Dakota canter the course Mona had set out for them. It had been three days since the hunter pace, and Christina wanted to show Mona what Sterling could do.

Katie turned to look at Christina worriedly. "How much higher?"

"Just a hole or two," Christina said, referring to the holes in the jump standards that kept the jump cups in place. Mona's course was set up so that the poles rested in their cups at three feet, or three feet three inches at the most. Christina wanted to jump three feet six inches at least; better yet, three feet nine inches.

"I don't know. Seabreeze is kind of quiet today. He feels tired." Katie twirled a piece of the bay's mane around her finger. "Why don't you wait until Seabreeze and I go one more time?"

Christina agreed, but inside she was wondering if Katie was really as serious as she was about riding. It made Christina a little sad to be leaving her friend behind.

"Dakota is still holding back," Mona called as Dylan finished the course, cantering a small circle before dropping down to a walk. "You've got to keep him in front of your legs."

Mona meant that when Dylan squeezed, Dakota had to respond by moving forward. Christina never had trouble keeping Sterling in front of her legs. If anything, she sometimes felt Sterling was leaving *her* behind.

"I was trying to, but he keeps hanging back." Even though Dylan was patting Dakota's neck, Christina could see his jaw tightening with frustration.

Mona ran her hands down Dakota's legs, checking for heat or swelling. "He doesn't look sore." She put both hands on her back as she straightened, as though her own muscles were feeling sore. "Maybe his tentativeness is a carryover from the event when he got hurt."

Dylan sagged a little in the saddle. Christina knew he was still feeling guilty for being so wrapped up with playing on the all-star soccer team that he hadn't given Dakota a safe ride over the cross-country or stadium phases of their last event. Dakota had ended up with a cut that needed stitches. But he was all healed now—on the outside at least.

"Dakota jumped fine at the hunt races, though," Dylan said.

Mona nodded. "But there he was jumping in the company of other horses." She put her hand on Dylan's knee. "If it's a confidence issue, don't worry about it. We'll just be sure not to overface him for a couple of months. By spring he'll be carrying you to the fences again, instead of you feeling like you're carrying him."

After Katie and Seabreeze jumped, Christina made her pitch. "Can you raise the jumps for Sterling? She did a lot of the training-level fences at the hunter pace."

"I'll help put them up," Dylan said, already swinging off Dakota's back.

"Me too," Christina added, shooting Dylan a smile of thanks.

Katie kicked her feet out of the stirrups. "Me three."

"Okay, okay. I can see I'm outnumbered." Mona raised her hands over her head, laughing.

When the poles were set and Christina was re-mounted, Mona called from the center of the ring.

"I want you to think about bending Sterling through the turns so she won't get fast and jump flat. Remember: *dressage over fences*."

"Okay," Christina said, pushing Sterling into a collected trot. She stayed on a circle until Sterling's back was soft and round.

When Christina asked her to canter, the mare's whole front end lifted as she went into the rocking horse movement. Sterling didn't pull at the bit, but her power bubbled beneath Christina, waiting to be unleashed.

"Be good, now," Christina whispered as they opened out and approached the first fence.

Sterling was all business, sailing over each jump, listening to Christina's half-halts at each turn. When they landed after the last fence, Christina rode a twenty-meter circle before dropping back to a walk and throwing her arms around Sterling's neck. "You are fantastic."

Christina had just straightened and was turning to the others when Mona's little dog, Muffin, came scooting under the fence. Sterling jumped six feet to the left, pivoting in the air so she landed facing the dog.

Mona laughed. "That was beautiful."

"The jumps or the shy?" Dylan asked, joking.

Mona ignored him. "She's listening so well, Christina. All your hard work is paying off."

"Does this mean I can move her up to training level for the Meadowlark Acres event?" Christina could hardly wait.

But Mona shook her head. "I'd like to see you two with one more novice event under your belt—or girth," she added with a chuckle.

"Telephone!" Sarah Stewart, Mona's assistant, yelled from the house.

"Good lesson, everyone," Mona said over her shoulder as she jogged away. "Next time we'll work on dressage."

"Bummer," Christina mumbled as she followed Katie and Dylan into the Gardener barn. She felt like hanging around to talk.

"Well, at least you'll be riding novice with Dylan and me," Katie pointed out.

"I know," Christina said. "I just feel bad for Sterling. She'll be bored."

"Sterling probably won't even notice," Dylan said, slipping off Dakota's bridle. Dylan let Dakota rub his head against his shoulder before putting a leather halter on him and fastening the crossties.

Christina disagreed. "You didn't see her jump at the hunter pace." She led Sterling into a nearby stall and began to massage her forehead with little circular motions. Sterling sighed and closed her eyes.

"No, but I've sure heard enough about it," Dylan said.

"You sound mad that I went." She rested her hands against Sterling's nose.

Dylan lifted the flap of his saddle and unfastened the girth before he answered. "Not really," he said finally. "But you didn't have to have such a good time."

Christina remembered their promise. "It was fun," she said, thinking how exhilarating it had been to gallop the big fences with Parker. "But I would rather have ridden with you," she quickly added, trying to sound convincing.

"Are you two at it again?" Cassidy Smith came out of the tack room with a saddle under one arm and a grooming kit under the other.

"Hi, Cass. When did you get back?" Katie called from the crossties at the end of the barn.

"Late last night. Mom let me sleep in a little before driving me to school today. I had to spend the day in the guidance office making up the tests I missed."

Christina listened with interest to the tall blond girl who, at thirteen, was already traveling up and down the East Coast competing in big, A-rated shows.

"Any news yet about what will happen to Rebound and Welly?" Christina asked, referring to Cassidy's Canadian warmblood jumper and Thoroughbred hunter. Cassidy's father had been unfairly accused of killing three racehorses and had his trainer's license revoked. Ever since then, money had been tight in Cassidy's family. Unless her father got his license back soon, Cassidy thought she might have to sell her two show horses to help her family out.

"Everything's pretty much the same," Cassidy said. Her face brightened when she added, "I made some extra money while I was away this time, though, showing some horses for a man whose regular rider got injured."

"You're a catch rider?" Christina was impressed. "Now you're really a professional."

"Hey, you should get Christina to introduce you to Parker Townsend," Katie said. She was always trying to get Cassidy paired up with someone. "He's a sopho-more at the high school. And he's a really good rider. Cassidy and Parker would make a great couple, wouldn't they?" she added, turning to Dylan and Christina.

Christina nodded. The thought of Parker and Cassidy together bothered her, although she would never admit it.

Cassidy balanced her saddle on a stall door. "I've already told you I don't have time to date," she reminded Katie.

"But you can ride together," Katie pointed out. "And he's really cute."

"Parker's not that new guy from England, is he?" Cassidy asked. "My brother, Campbell, says the girls are falling all over him because of his accent."

"He's the one," Christina said. "Only he's an American. He has an accent from going to school over there."

Cassidy grinned. "Campbell told us about him at dinner one night. That kid sounds crazy."

"You can say that again." Dylan glanced at Christina.

"What did he do?" Christina asked, smoothing Sterling's mane to one side while the mare dozed.

Cassidy laughed. "Campbell said Parker borrowed a friend's motorcycle and rode it through the high school."

"You're kidding," Dylan said.

"No, really. He got someone to open the front door,

and he rode right down the main hall, up a flight of stairs, through Campbell's biology class, and out through the greenhouse. It took them a while to figure out who did it because Parker's helmet hid his face."

Dylan shook his head. "I wonder how he managed the stairs."

Katie had moved up to listen. "I bet he got in big trouble."

"Three days' suspension. And this is the guy you want me to date? Ha!" Cassidy went into Rebound's stall, then peeked back over the door. "There are rumors that he may have been the one who put the PE teacher's boxer shorts on top of the flagpole, too."

Christina laughed. She could just see Parker shinnying up the pole.

"That guy is bad news," Dylan said. "You should have seen the way he rode at the hunt races."

"He beat you, huh?" Cassidy grinned.

Dylan tossed a brush into his kit. "I didn't care about that. It was just the way he pushed his horse. He jumped those hedges like he had a death wish."

"It wasn't that bad," Christina said. "Foxy knew what she was doing. You should see this mare, Cassidy. She's amazing."

"Well, I still think he's crazy," Dylan said, unsnapping Dakota's crossties.

Christina thought the stories about school were pretty funny. It wasn't as though anyone had gotten hurt. She didn't want to argue with Dylan, though.

As Christina rode Sterling home to Whitebrook through the woods, a disturbing thought crossed her mind. What if Parker went too far and got thrown out of this school, too? Would he be sent away again?

On Friday afternoon after school Christina and Melanie hacked over to Whisperwood Farm to spend the night, since Ashleigh and Mike were out of town at a sale.

"Soda or milk with dinner?" Samantha asked.

Melanie and Christina grinned at each other. Ashleigh never gave them that choice. "Soda," they said in unison.

Samantha had rented a movie that turned out to be pretty scary. The three of them were huddled on the sofa under a blanket, eating popcorn together, when Samantha screamed. Christina and Melanie leaped up, sending popcorn flying in all directions.

"Sorry," a deep voice said. Tor was backing away and rubbing his cheek.

Christina hadn't noticed Tor come in the door behind the couch, either. When he had bent down to kiss Samantha, she had reacted instinctively, clobbering him in self-defense.

"No, *I'm* sorry." Samantha giggled as she smoothed the side of his face. "I didn't know it was you."

Tor laughed. "Who did you think I was?"

"The creep in the movie," Melanie said, as though it were perfectly obvious.

Christina and Melanie salvaged the popcorn as Samantha went with Tor to find an ice pack. Melanie checked a piece before tossing it into her mouth. "Samantha's more fun than most grown-ups."

"Yeah," Christina said. "I know what you mean."

Kevin came over to Whisperwood the following morning, and he, Melanie, and Tor went off on a trail ride. Christina stayed with Samantha to help her school one of the young horses over some cross-country fences. Christina rode Sterling over the fences, too. She figured every bit of training helped.

"This is great," Samantha said. She was riding a Connemara gelding named Apple Butter for his golden dun coloring. "He's only here for a month of training, so I want to give him as much mileage as I can."

They took turns popping over logs and easy jumps. Sometimes Samantha led the way, and sometimes she asked Christina to take Sterling over first. "I hate to see a horse that always has to be in front," Samantha said.

They left one field, cutting through a patch of woods to another field where the more advanced course was. Samantha wanted Christina to see the jumps.

"Not that you and Sterling are ready for them yet," Samantha cautioned.

"But Sterling and I jumped most of the training-level fences at River Oaks last weekend."

"I know you're eager," Samantha said, sounding

just like Mona. "But don't take too many chances. Even though Sterling is a brave and lovely jumper, she's still green. And green horses make mistakes." Samantha gave her a long look. "If Sterling makes her mistakes over smaller fences, she'll be more likely to come out unharmed and smarter for it."

Christina knew that Sterling didn't have as much experience as some horses, but she thought Samantha was making her sound less trained than she really was. After all, didn't talent count for anything?

Both horses' heads went up and Sterling whinnied as they came out of the woods overlooking a rolling field. A large bay was galloping across the grass.

Samantha shaded her eyes with one hand. "Isn't that Parker?"

Christina smiled at the tall, slightly bent form. "Yep," she said, hoping Samantha wouldn't notice that her cheeks were getting pink.

They watched as he circled the field, soaring over solid fences built out of whole tree trunks. Christina bet that the jumps would be up to her shoulders if she stood by them.

"I wish I could have brought that mare home," Samantha said with a sigh. "She sure is a bold jumper."

"She and Parker are a good match, though," Christina said. "I told him he should take up eventing."

"He can ride, all right," Samantha admitted. "But he shouldn't be taking fences like this without someone around in case anything happens." She trotted

Apple Butter down the hill, with Christina following.

When Parker spotted them, he rode over right away. "Hi, Christina," he said, looking really happy to see her.

"Hi, Parker." Christina grinned back. She'd been wondering when she would see him again.

"Parker Townsend," he said, sticking out his hand to Samantha. "You probably don't remember me, Mrs. Nelson. I hope you don't mind my crossing your land."

"Call me Samantha," Sam said, returning his handshake. "I don't mind people riding on our land as long as they close the gates, but I am concerned that you're jumping without anyone watching."

"I understand completely. It's just that when I saw these fantastic jumps, I couldn't resist." When Parker grinned that way, it was impossible not to smile back. "Christina told me you're a big-time event rider."

"I don't know about the big-time part," Samantha said, giving Christina a sidelong glance. "But I had a chance to ride in a couple of four-star events in Britain."

"I was thinking about entering Foxy in the Meadowlark event, even though I haven't worked much with her in dressage."

"You are?" Christina said, suddenly looking forward to the event even more. "I am, too. And so are Dylan and Katie."

"Maybe we could work out a deal," Samantha said to Parker. "If you give Tor a hand around here building new jumps on weekends, I'll help you get Foxy started with dressage."

"Would you?" Parker said, his eyes opening wide. "That would be great!"

"Make sure it's okay with your parents, though. Stop by sometime and we'll put you to work. Speaking of which," Samantha added, nodding to Christina, "we'd better get going. I've got three more horses to ride."

Christina reluctantly followed Samantha back up the path they'd just come down. As they started into the woods, she turned back in time to see Parker jump a big triple bar with a boxed ditch underneath called a coffin, giving a war whoop as he galloped away.

Samantha shook her head. "There's a thin line between nerve and foolishness."

But Christina was smiling as she watched Parker and Foxy disappear over the stone wall that made up the boundary of the Nelsons' farm.

When Christina called Katie Wednesday night with a question about the English project they were working on together, Katie said, "I was going to call *you*. You'll never guess what Cassidy told me at the barn today."

Christina flopped back on her bed, ready to hear the latest gossip. "What?"

"Parker Townsend has entered his horse in the *training*-level division instead of novice at Meadowlark, even though it's their first event."

"He did?" Christina said, sitting up again.

"I told her Parker is crazy. He's going to get himself killed."

Christina was surprised to hear Katie sounding like such a worrywart. She was as bad as Mona and Samantha. "I don't know," Christina said, coming to Parker's defense. "He's a really good rider, and it's only training level."

"*Only* training level?" Katie said. "Those jumps scare me to death."

"Well, I think they're fun." Christina was getting tired of hearing people talk as though jumping was so dangerous. "And he has two and a half more weeks to get Foxy ready, anyway."

"What do you mean? The event's a week from Saturday."

The calendar over Christina's bed was still turned to the old month. "No, it isn't," she said, flipping up the page. As her eyes scanned the calendar squares, her stomach dropped. "My gosh, you're right. And I haven't even mailed in my entry yet."

As soon as they got off the phone, Christina rummaged around her desk and found the form. Luckily, she hadn't missed the closing date to enter. Even so, she filled out the information right away and went downstairs to get an envelope and a check from her mother.

"Thanks, Mom," Christina said as Ashleigh finished signing the permission part of the slip. "Do we have any stamps?"

"Top right desk drawer," her mother answered. "If

you leave the envelope with my pile of bills, I'll mail it tomorrow."

It wasn't until Christina turned off the light to go to bed that she started thinking about Parker going at training level instead of novice with her, Katie, and Dylan. Christina knew that he and Foxy could jump the fences, no problem. Their dressage probably wouldn't be very good, though. Sterling was a lot more ready to go training level than Foxy—after all, she had more dressage experience.

But Parker would be jumping the exciting fences while Christina was stuck with the boring low ones. The more Christina thought about the event, the madder she got about the way Mona was holding her back. Sterling was Christina's horse, and she knew in her heart that they were ready for the challenge.

So what was stopping her?

Christina jumped out of bed and tiptoed downstairs to retrieve the entry form and a new envelope and stamp. When she was safely back in her room, she found her bottle of correction fluid in the inside pocket of her backpack. Christina hunched over her desk, carefully whiting out "Novice" and blowing on it until the fluid was dry. With a determined hand, she printed "Training" in its place. Then she refolded the entry form, slid it into the new envelope with the check, and crept downstairs to leave it on the stack of mail her mother would take to the post office the next day.

As Christina was about to turn off the light again,

she spotted the old envelope torn open on her desk. Just to be on the safe side, she stuffed it into her backpack to throw away at school.

When Christina snuggled back under her comforter, she was sure she'd done the right thing.

8

FOR THE NEXT SEVERAL DAYS, CHRISTINA WENT BACK AND forth about whether she should tell Dylan and Katie what she'd done. Every time they talked about the event, Christina chickened out. Katie would just fuss at her, and Dylan would think she'd changed her entry because of Parker—which was true in a way. Parker had shown her how much she and Sterling could already do. But Dylan might not understand that. What if he accused her of having a crush on Parker? Christina wouldn't know what to say.

On Friday afternoon after school, the day before the event, Ashleigh dropped Christina, Dylan, Parker, and Katie off at Meadowlark Acres so that they could walk the cross-country course. Christina's stomach was tied up in knots. As soon as her friends picked up their maps and programs, her secret would be out.

"I'm going to jog the course three times," Dylan said as they headed up the stairs of the farmhouse porch to pick up their packets. At the last event, when Dakota had been injured, Dylan hadn't even walked the course once.

"That's good," Katie said. "Dakota wouldn't appreciate wiping out again."

Parker laced his fingers together, stretching out his arms and cracking his knuckles in anticipation. "It's too bad we can't take the horses for a trial run."

"But then it wouldn't be as exciting," Christina said. "The whole idea is that all the horses ride a course they've never seen before. It really tests how much they trust their riders."

A girl in breeches and running shoes gave them each a large manila envelope with a number pinny and program inside. She went out on the porch with them and pointed to the field where the cross-country started.

"If you want, you can stick your envelopes in the shed beside the starting box while you walk the course. You two"—the girl pointed to Dylan and Katie—"should follow the black numbers on white flags. Those are the novice jumps. And you guys," she added, nodding in Christina and Parker's direction, "will jump the fences with the white-on-black flags."

Katie nudged Christina with her elbow as the girl went back in the house. "She thinks you're going training, too."

Christina waited until they were away from the porch before she said, "I am."

"What?" Dylan looked at her as though he hadn't heard right.

"I decided to go training level after all," Christina said, trying to sound as if it was no big deal.

"Did Mona say you could?" Katie asked.

Christina kept walking. "She doesn't know."

"You're kidding!" When Christina looked back, Katie was standing with her mouth open.

But Parker laughed. "What's the problem? It's not as if Sterling hasn't already jumped training-level fences."

Dylan ignored him. "So what about your mom and dad? They said it's okay?"

"Not exactly," Christina admitted. "I didn't ask."

"That's the way," Parker said, his gray eyes sparkling as though he and Christina were sharing something special. "Never let parents have the upper hand. They don't know everything."

"That's right," Christina said, her confidence flowing back. "I'm the one who's training Sterling, anyway, so I should get to decide."

Dylan and Katie didn't say anything, but Christina didn't like the way they looked at each other. She pretended nothing was wrong, though, pulling out the map and studying the course as she walked. When she glanced out the corner of her eye, Dylan and Katie were doing the same. Parker jogged ahead to check out the starting box.

Christina was the first to break the silence. "The novice and training courses split after the first jump."

"Yeah, I see that," Katie said.

"I guess I'll go ahead, then. Meet you at the box when we're done?" Christina suggested.

"Sure." For a second it seemed as if Dylan wanted to add more.

When he shut his mouth instead, Christina blurted out, "Look, I'm sorry I didn't tell you guys before. I don't know why I didn't."

Katie chewed the inside of her mouth. "Well, I hope you know what you're doing," she finally said.

"You won't tell my mom, will you?" Christina demanded.

Dylan snorted. "She's going to find out tomorrow anyway. And when Mona comes back from Pennsylvania next week, she's going to flip."

"I know. But I'll think of something by then." Christina wished Dylan would look at her. When he didn't, she turned and jogged to where Parker was waiting.

She cheered up once they began walking the course and studying the fences. Most of the jumps were big and solid but not too tricky. As they headed toward the tenth fence—a stone wall—Christina was already planning how she could let Sterling open up into a real gallop after the ninth jump, since there was a whole hayfield to cross before they got to the next obstacle.

"Come check this one out," Parker said, stopping to admire a fence halfway down the field to the left, even though it wasn't part of their course. "It's awesome," he added, starting to sound more like an American kid again.

Christina followed Parker as he walked to the jump for a closer look. It was at least an intermediate-level fence—maybe advanced—built into the wall of an old, empty hay barn. The doors on both ends had been completely removed so that a horse could canter through the building and jump out on the other side. Because the barn was built into a bank, the floor was at eye level as Christina stood below the door. She tilted her head back to look at the hay manger the horse had to jump to leave the barn. It was at least an eight-foot drop to where they were standing.

"I'm not crazy about drop fences," Christina admitted. "My brain gets mixed up when it takes longer to land on the downhill side. It's like missing a step when I'm going down a flight of stairs in the dark."

"That's what makes it so great," Parker said. His eyes were wide, but Christina felt he was looking right through her. "Jumping that fence would be like flying."

Maybe someday, Christina thought, *but not yet.* "Come on," she said to Parker. "I want to go over the course a couple of times so Sterling and I won't mess up."

"You worry too much," Parker teased. He gave the barn jump a last, lingering look before jogging over to Christina.

112

"Were you really planning to be a jockey?" she asked as they approached the stone wall.

"That's what I wanted to do," Parker said. "Not that my mother would have let me. I was going to wait until I was eighteen."

Christina was surprised. "What does she have against racing, anyway?" It seemed strange since the Townsends bred racehorses.

"Nothing," Parker said, adding in a snooty voice, "as long as no one in the family associates with the lower ranks."

"So jockeys aren't high-class enough?" Christina felt the back of her neck start to prickle as she imagined Lavinia looking down her nose at Ashleigh.

"I didn't say that." Parker walked backward so that he could face her. "I'd do anything to be able to ride races. But my mother has other ideas. She wants me to study finance or law. That's why she shipped me to England to go to school—so I could be chums with all the future barons and barristers."

"Who?"

"Sons of nobility, or at least their solicitors. Lawyers," Parker added when he saw Christina's confusion. "They only let blue bloods in my school—and rich Americans. But instead of hobnobbing with their families and making the right connections, like my mother wanted," Parker said, putting on his snooty voice again, "I spent as much time as I could with my grandfather's racehorses."

"Riding?"

"Riding, grooming, mucking out, you name it. When I was around the horses, I wasn't as homesick." Parker was quiet for a few steps. When he continued, his voice was so soft that Christina had to drift closer to hear.

"When my mother finally figured out that I wasn't, as she put it, paving my way into the right society, she forbid me to go to the stables for holidays anymore. That's when I borrowed the Mini-Cooper," Parker finished, shoving his hands into his pockets.

So that was the rest of the story, Christina thought as they climbed over the next two fences, figuring out the best way to approach them. They headed silently down the hill. Then Christina broke the stillness. "Do you miss England now?" she asked.

"Are you kidding?" Parker said, turning an astonished face toward her. "I never wanted to leave Kentucky in the first place."

Parker didn't talk much the rest of the way through the course. It was as though he had gone inside himself and shut the door. Christina was glad to meet up with the others at the end.

On the way home in the car, Dylan and Katie didn't spill the beans about Christina's changing her entry. They didn't have much to say, though. Not that any of them could have gotten a word in edgewise, since Parker had opened up again and was giving Ashleigh a blow-by-blow description of the jumps. As Christina watched Parker's animated face she got the feeling he was performing. Now that she had glimpsed another side of him, this bright, sparkly Parker seemed fake.

They dropped Parker off last. "You can let me out here," he said when they pulled into the gate of Townsend Acres. He jumped out of the car, bending over to repeat his thanks to Ashleigh and waving as they backed out into the road.

Christina watched him walk toward the beautiful white Colonial house sitting by itself on a rise. Its long green lawn looked as though bicycles or toys had never trampled its perfect blades.

"What was living at Townsend Acres like?" she asked her mother as they drove away.

"It's a beautiful farm," Ashleigh said.

Christina heard the uncertainty in her mother's voice. "But?" she pressed.

Ashleigh sighed. "But it wasn't ours. I was just the barn manager's daughter, and Brad Townsend made sure I didn't forget it. Every time I felt good about Wonder or some other horse I was working with, Brad was always there to put me down."

"I feel sorry for Parker, having a father like Brad," Christina said.

Ashleigh's laugh was hollow. "Lavinia's no picnic either. Sometimes I think Parker's better off away from them at school." She pressed her lips together and glanced at Christina. "I shouldn't be saying bad things about Lavinia and Brad. Please don't repeat them."

Dusk was falling as they turned up Whitebrook's driveway. Christina loved the way the white crisscross fence opened to the old farmhouse with its wraparound porch and the three big barns where her father, Melanie, Kevin, and all the other people who felt more like family than hired hands were settling the horses in for the night.

Christina couldn't imagine ever leaving Whitebrook. Her parents would never send her away from home the way Parker's parents had. They'd miss her too much.

She hoped they'd still feel that way after the Meadowlark event the next day.

"Where are my stupid boot pulls?" Christina said at the event the next morning as she dumped the contents of her gym bag out on the floor of the trailer's dressing room. "I was sure I packed them last night."

"Here. Use mine," Katie said, handing her a pair of long silver hooks with wooden handles.

"Thanks," Christina said, sitting on a tack trunk. She slid the hooks through the loops on the inside of her tall black riding boots and started to pull them on over her cream breeches. "Auuuugh," she groaned when her toe touched the shoe tree she'd forgotten to pull out of the foot of the boot.

"Why are you so uptight?" Katie asked, coming to the rescue by pulling Christina's half-on boot back off

116

again. "You don't usually get this nervous at shows."

"I'm not nervous," Christina said. "I'm just in a hurry. Sterling needs a lot of time to warm up before her dressage test." She was lying about being nervous. Now that the event was here, Christina was worried about having signed up for training level. Was her mother going to be mad when she found out? Or worse, would Christina and Sterling get hurt in the cross-country?

Katie had ridden her dressage test earlier, and now she was pulling a green and purple jersey over her head for cross-country. "I wish I could watch your dressage test," Katie said. "But while you're cantering circles, Seabreeze will be running away with me on cross-country."

That made Christina laugh. "The only thing Bree has ever run away from is work."

"That's what cross-country is," Katie said, bending to fasten small silver spurs onto her boots. "By the time we get around the course, my legs will be ready to drop off from pushing so hard."

There was a knock on the dressing room door. When Christina opened it, Dylan and Sterling peered in.

"Sterling wants to know when you're coming out to play," Dylan joked.

"I'm all set," Christina said, buttoning her black hunt coat. "Thanks for holding her for me."

Dylan hung on to the right side stirrup so that the saddle wouldn't shift to the left while Christina mounted. "I'm going to get changed for cross-country now, but I'll try to watch your test before Dakota and I head over to the field."

"Okay," Christina said. "If I don't get a chance to talk to you before you go, good luck."

Dylan's eyes crinkled as he grinned up at her. "You too."

Christina's stomach hopped, but this time it wasn't from nerves.

Sterling lifted her head and whinnied hello to Foxy as Parker rode up.

It was the first time Christina had seen him that day and she was relieved; now she had someone to back her up when her mother found out she was riding Training level. Ashleigh had offered to give Parker and Foxy a ride to the event, but Parker's grandfather had wanted to drive them over himself in the Townsend Acres van.

"Good day," Parker said, sweeping off his black velvet hunt cap. His dark hair curled up along the sides where the hat had been.

What is wrong with me? Christina thought as she felt a current run through her body. *One second I decide Dylan's the one, but then Parker comes along and mixes me up again.*

When Parker turned to Dylan, he switched back to a more normal voice. "How'd your test go?"

"No complaints." Dylan touched Christina's boot. "Got to run."

"Bye." Christina waited until Dylan disappeared into the trailer before turning back to Parker and gathering Sterling's reins. "Is Foxy warmed up yet?"

"I've done a little bit," Parker said, shrugging. "She gets bored with too much flat work."

Sterling danced sideways as a horse trotted past. Her whole rib cage expanded when she whinnied again. Christina laughed, shaking her head at Sterling's excitement. "*Someone* needs reminding about why we're here."

Parker moved Foxy closer. "Did your mother find out yet?" he asked in a conspiratorial voice.

Christina shook her head, glancing to where Ashleigh was talking to an old friend. "I don't think she's seen a program yet."

A horse cantered too close to Foxy, who showed her displeasure by rearing and spinning around, almost bumping into Sterling. "Hey," Christina said, moving Sterling out of the way.

Foxy's front legs barely touched the ground before she stretched her head down and bucked. Parker laughed as he sat back, kicking her forward into a canter. Christina watched Parker circle, gradually coaxing Foxy into a dressage frame. She had to smile. Boy, could he ride.

By the time the judge rang the little bell signaling that it was time for Christina to enter the dressage arena, Sterling had gotten used to the noise and activity around her. Her mother waved, mouthing "Good luck" from the sidelines. Dylan gave her a thumbs-up as he sat on Dakota in the warm-up area.

Christina took a deep breath, focusing on the test ahead. "Okay, girl. Do your stuff." Sterling whinnied one last time to Dakota before answering Christina's half-halt by lowering her head and softly mouthing the bit.

When they turned at the A marker and trotted down the center line, Sterling lifted her back and began to lengthen her stride. *Not now,* Christina thought, smiling for the judge through clenched teeth as she closed her legs and hands, sitting back and asking Sterling to slow down. The mare halted at X, snapping to attention as Christina dropped one hand to her side and bowed her head in salute to the judge. When Sterling went from her halt right into a springy trot, Christina smiled for real. Sterling was ready to shine.

Christina remembered to sit up straight, using her back and stomach muscles to sit to Sterling's trot. When she moved her leg behind the girth and asked for a canter, Sterling lifted her back and settled into a rocking-horse gait. And when it was time to come back to a trot, it felt as though Sterling's legs had stretched six inches as Christina asked for a lengthening across the diagonal. By the time they halted at G, right in front of the judge, Christina was so proud of her mare, she thought she'd burst.

"Good girl," she said as they left the ring on a long rein, her hand stroking Sterling's neck just below the mare's neat black braids. "You are the best horse ever."

"That was wonderful, honey," her mother said,

meeting them outside the arena. "I can't believe that this is the same mare that couldn't canter a twenty-meter circle last spring without thinking she had to go faster so she wouldn't fall down."

"Yeah," Christina said, beaming. "She really has come a long way."

Parker was entering the ring now, so Christina and her mom turned to watch.

"That mare has lovely gaits," Ashleigh observed during the test. "Parker doesn't have her as round and collected as Sterling, but she's moving quite nicely."

Christina agreed. If not for the buck in the middle of Foxy's first canter circle, and breaking into a canter both times that Parker asked her to lengthen in the trot, it would have been a nice test.

As it was, Parker didn't seem at all bothered by the mare's performance. He patted her hindquarters, then swung his leg over the saddle the second they left the dressage arena. "Race time," he said, hitching his shoulders up and down and grinning at Christina.

His excitement was infectious. "Come on, Sterling," she said to her mare. "Let's get ready for some real action."

9

AN HOUR LATER CHRISTINA DID A FINAL CHECK TO MAKE sure that Sterling was all set for cross-country. The mare's braids had been taken out, leaving Sterling's mane in a curly fringe on her neck. The lower portion of her long black legs was protected by red splint boots whose padding could save Sterling from cutting herself if she slipped or had an accident. Red rubber bell boots were fastened over her front hooves for protection, too.

Christina closed the Velcro on the safety vest that fit snugly over her red and white striped jersey. The dense, half-inch foam would protect her if she fell off and Sterling stepped or rolled on her, not that she expected any of these things to happen. Then she grabbed her leather gloves—a necessity with Sterling, whose her neck got so wet with sweat that sometimes that it was hard to hold on to the reins. She was just checking Sterling's girth one more time when she heard her mother call her name. As soon as Christina turned around, she knew she was in big trouble.

Ashleigh's jaw was tight as she waved the program. "Who said you could go training level?"

Christina swallowed. "No one. I decided myself." She straightened her shoulders, looking down at her mother.

"Even after Mona specifically told you she wanted Sterling to go novice one more time?" Ashleigh's hazel eyes were boring into hers.

She should have known that Mona would tell her mother everything. That was the problem when your mother and your riding instructor were best friends.

"But Sterling can do it. I know she can," Christina said. "You should have seen her at the hunter pace."

When Ashleigh folded her arms and looked away, Christina could see the muscles in her neck tensing. "I should make you load her on the trailer right now for disobeying Mona and me."

The words were like a slap in the face as Christina realized her mother was serious. She tried to swallow, but her mouth was too dry. "I didn't disobey you. You never said I couldn't go training level, and Mona was just *suggesting* I stay in novice." Before the words were out of her mouth, Christina knew she'd said the wrong thing.

Ashleigh was frowning even more when she turned back. "What was on the entry form when I signed it?"

"Novice," Christina admitted. "But I didn't plan it that way. I just changed my mind after you signed it."

Ashleigh looked as though she didn't believe her.

"It's true," Christina said, her voice trembling. "I'm not lying to you. Everyone keeps telling me what to do with Sterling without listening to what I have to say at all. And I'm the one who knows her the best."

Sterling nuzzled Christina's cheek, gently blowing into her face.

"You more than anyone should know how I feel, Mom," Christina continued, gathering strength from Sterling's sweet, grassy breath. "When everyone else thought Wonder wasn't good enough to race, you knew her well enough to see that she could be a champion. And you kept trying." Christina was grasping at straws, but she hoped her mother would remember how she had felt when she was thirteen.

"That was different," Ashleigh said. "I was working with a trainer." Her face got sad, and Christina knew she was thinking about Charlie Burke, the old man who had helped her become a successful jockey. Her mother had a framed picture of the two of them on her desk.

"But weren't there times when you didn't agree with Charlie? Didn't you sometimes know in your heart what was best for Wonder?"

Ashleigh closed her eyes for a long moment. Christina bit her lower lip as she waited. Finally her mother sighed and looked at her.

"I'll let you do it on one condition."

Christina heart fluttered. "Anything."

Her mother reached out, resting her hand on Christina's arm. "I want you to *promise* me that you won't go too fast. If you'll keep Sterling at novice speed instead of pushing her to make the training-level time, you may ride."

Christina rubbed Sterling's nose. Even though she'd dreamed of flying around the course and coming in with no jumping or time penalties, she could see that her mom was offering her a fair deal. "I promise."

Ashleigh nodded. "The most important thing right now is to give Sterling a safe ride. We'll talk more about your subterfuge later."

"Okay." Christina stood for a second, then took a step toward her mother, who swept her into a big hug. "I'm sorry."

Ashleigh rubbed her back. "Just don't let anything happen to my little girl or your horse," she whispered.

Even though Christina knew she wasn't out of hot water yet with her mother and Mona, she felt a lot lighter when she swung up into the saddle and headed down the road to the cross-country field. Sterling was keyed up, shying at a weed waving in the breeze, and jumping when a robin flew in front of her.

"Will you please stop that?" Christina said when Sterling ducked sideways to slink past an old paper bag that lay crumpled in the dirt path. "You're starting to make *me* nervous."

Once they got to the warm-up area, where they

could canter, Sterling began to relax. Christina loved the way the mare blew air out of her nose with each stride, making it easy to settle into a rhythm. After jumping the cross-rail and oxer practice fences a few times, Christina pulled Sterling back to a walk so that she could watch a few riders starting and finishing cross-country.

The course consisted of seventeen jumps, but since they were spread out across a mile and a half of fields and woods, she could see only three of them from the warm-up area. Christina flexed her fingers as she watched a rider decked out in green and black leave the starting box. She couldn't wait until she and Sterling were the ones galloping across the grass, jumping fences under the admiring gazes of the volunteer judges, one at each fence, who recorded the horses as they went over each obstacle. Her mother and Mr. Townsend had already left the starting area, walking to a spot on the course where they could watch Christina and Parker jump several of the fences.

"Dylan said your mom found out." Parker said as he brought Foxy up beside Sterling. "I bet she was in a dander."

Christina laughed at his English slang. "A little," she admitted. "But she's letting us go anyway. How's Foxy?"

The big bay mare had flecks of foam dripping from her mouth already. Parker must have put her through a pretty thorough warm-up. Not that Foxy acted tired.

She jigged impatiently beside Sterling before finally rearing halfway up and spinning.

Parker grinned as he brought her back around again, his seat never leaving the saddle. "You'd better set a good pace or we'll catch up to you before the wall." Parker was slated to leave the box three minutes after Christina.

"Number seventeen, you're on deck," a man called. Christina didn't have time to explain that she'd promised her mother she'd stick to a novice pace.

"That's me. Wish us luck," Christina said nervously, gathering up her reins. Sterling raised her head and broke into a trot.

"Break a leg," Parker said, as if Christina were going onstage. "No, on second thought, better not," he quickly corrected himself.

Christina stuck her tongue out at him. She could hear him laughing as they headed to the start.

"Not yet," Christina told Sterling as the mare started to duck into the starting box. She knew from experience that Sterling got fidgety if she took her in too soon. It wasn't until the person with the stopwatch began the ten-second countdown that Christina walked Sterling into the square, deliberately positioning her so the mare's tail was toward the first jump.

". . . two, one . . ."

Christina turned Sterling around. Before she could even close her legs on the mare's sides, Sterling leaped into a canter and headed to the first fence.

"Easy," Christina said, opening and closing her fingers on the reins until Sterling had settled back into a balanced canter. Four strides later, Sterling sailed over the dark brown coop. Christina's heart was sailing, too. They were off!

She kept her seat low in the saddle and her hands steady on either side of Sterling's neck as they galloped away from the jump. The mare's front legs reached out further and further until it felt as if they were flying over the grass. "All right," Christina said, the wind snatching away her words.

Sterling's head came up as she looked for the next fence, her hooves drumming on. As Christina felt the mare's heart pounding under her legs, she reminded herself to breathe. It was easy to forget in all the excitement, and the last thing Christina needed was to get light-headed from holding her breath.

They veered to the right and approached the hanging log jump. "Steady, now," Christina said, sitting back and riding a half-halt to collect Sterling before the fence.

Sterling's rhythm didn't change as she shortened her stride, her chest coming up like the bow of a boat as she rebalanced herself. Even so, they got in a little too close to the jump, causing Sterling to rock back on her haunches and catapult over the massive timber. Christina was nearly unseated in the process.

That was a close one, Christina thought, fumbling for her lost stirrup as Sterling charged up the hill. Her toe caught hold of it again just in time for Christina to lock her calves against Sterling's sides as they soared over the birch tree gate. The ski ramp was next, an angled black platform on the edge of a hill. Christina braced herself for the drop on the other side, but Sterling got over it with no problem.

Jumps five, six, and seven were straightforward, but Sterling's pace accelerated with each one. Fence eight, truck and tractor tires standing on end like a stack of doughnuts turned sideways, nearly left Christina in the dirt once again when Sterling, suspicious of the black rubber, took off too early and jumped as though she were crossing an alligator-filled stream.

"We've got to slow down," Christina said, fighting to bring Sterling back to an organized canter. The close call had reminded her of the promise she'd made to her mother. Sterling settled back, but Christina knew from the feel of the tight muscles under the saddle that it was just a matter of time before Sterling exploded.

And she did. Three strides before the cordwood fence, Sterling's nose shot into the air to avoid the bit. Christina's heart was in her throat as Sterling galloped the last two strides and launched herself at the solid stack of firewood that was lashed together with wire. If she hit it, they'd flip for sure.

Christina heard the fence judge gasp as they scrambled in the air. Instead of the horse lifting her knees and tucking her front hooves against her chest, Christina could feel that Sterling's legs were hanging dangerously behind. At the last minute, though, Sterling twisted her body and they made it over the big fence, landing with a teeth-jarring thud.

"That's it," Christina said, using one hand like a pulley as she brought Sterling back to a trot. They couldn't keep going until the mare was balanced and calmer.

Fortunately they were in the long, flat field with the hay barn. Christina couldn't even see jump ten at the far end because the field curved with the river. With no jump in sight ahead, Christina hoped she could get Sterling's attention back once and for all. She couldn't risk their necks by continuing before Sterling was settled and listening again.

Christina could see the veins standing out through the mare's thin skin as they trotted a dozen or more figure eights until Sterling finally softened her jaw and relaxed. "That's it," Christina cooed, reaching forward to stroke her sweaty neck. "I shouldn't have let you get so fired up."

She was just about to ask Sterling for a canter again when she heard hoofbeats approaching.

"Heads up," Parker called as Foxy blasted over the cordwood.

Christina was surprised. Parker must have been really flying to catch up with them this fast.

"Are you coming?" Parker said, pretending to tip his hat as they cantered past.

She could see the jump judge at the cordwood holding the walkie-talkie to her mouth, probably letting the technical delegate know that Parker had overtaken

Christina. "We can't. I have to let you pass."

"Last one back buys the soda," Parker said, waving as they galloped off, his bright yellow shirtsleeves rippling in the breeze. Sterling got excited again, eager to make a race of it, so Christina had to circle her two more times before continuing the course. When she looked up, Parker was already out of sight.

"Good girl," Christina said as they set off down the field in a reasonably collected hand gallop. The tension had gone out of Sterling's neck, and Christina was pleased that the mare felt lighter in her hands. As they started to pass the old hay barn with the scary drop jump, Christina caught a glimpse of yellow out of the corner of her eye. Sterling saw it, too, and swerved away.

"Oh, no," Christina muttered as she sat back in the saddle, closing her hands on the reins. The yellow disappeared around the barn. It was Parker.

"Don't!" she yelled when Foxy appeared in the far opening. But Christina knew in the pit of her stomach that it was too late. Parker was going to jump the drop.

It was illegal to jump any fences that weren't part of the course, but they were out of sight of the fence judges, so Parker probably figured nobody would find out. Or maybe he didn't care.

Foxy's head was up, as though she was hesitating, as Parker drove her into the shadowy barn. She kept cantering, but Christina could see her holding back, her body weaving as she switched leads.

The doorway with the jump looked enormous from Christina's viewpoint, even bigger than it had when they were walking the course. Foxy scrambled before it, peering over the hay manger as if she wasn't sure what was waiting for her in the long, waving grass below. When she finally took off, it was in slow motion.

Christina watched in horror as the mare's left front hoof caught the log that made up the far edge of the manger. Foxy's head lunged forward, pulling the reins free from Parker's hands as she tried to recover her balance, but it was hopeless. Her shoulder skidded along the log as her hindquarters came up. Parker shot over her neck into the grass below a second before Foxy flipped, tail over head, in a grotesque somersault. Christina gasped as the horse crashed to the ground. Foxy didn't move.

"Parker!" Christina screamed, imagining him crushed under Foxy's enormous body.

When Parker didn't answer, Christina didn't know what to do. Christina turned Sterling toward them, then decided she'd better get help first.

"Come on, girl," she said, pressing her heels into Sterling's sides. "It's time to run."

Sterling didn't need to be told twice. She bolted down the field toward the cordwood. Seconds later Christina was shouting at the startled jump judge.

"We need an ambulance at the hay barn. Hurry!" When the judge picked up the walkie-talkie, Christina wheeled Sterling back around and galloped back, praying with every stride that she'd find Parker and Foxy up.

They weren't, though Foxy twitched her ear as they approached. Christina's stomach sank when she saw Parker lying facedown, his legs pinned under Foxy's rib cage and his head dangerously close to Foxy's back legs. If the mare tried to stand, Parker could be kicked.

Christina vaulted out of the saddle, putting a hand on Sterling's neck to steady herself a second before throwing the reins over an old split-rail fence angled out from the bank barn. "You wait here," she commanded, giving Sterling's forehead a quick caress. "Be good. Don't pull back."

The long grass tore at her boots as she waded through it to Foxy, who was beginning to stir. "Easy," Christina murmured, squatting down and placing her knee across the mare's cheek and upper neck. She was careful to make sure she wasn't interfering with Foxy's breathing as she used her weight to keep the mare from trying to get up. Foxy would have to lift her head first to stand, and Christina had to keep that from happening.

"You're going to be okay, Parker," Christina said, watching his protective vest rise and fall as he breathed. "Can you hear me? Help is coming. Just keep still," she said, terrified tears rolling down her cheeks.

Parker didn't give any sign of hearing her, but Christina felt as though she had to keep talking or he might stop breathing.

"You and Foxy aren't afraid of anything, are you?"

she said, trying to smile through her tears as she stroked the mare's mane. "You're such a great team, I bet you'll beat us to the Olympics. Your parents will be so proud. Even your mom will be glad you kept riding." She tried not to wonder if Parker's neck was broken. If only he would move.

10

THE GRASS RUSTLED BEHIND HER. WHEN CHRISTINA LOOKED back, Sterling was pivoting around as a yellow and white ambulance came bumping across the field. A pickup truck followed in its wake.

"Over here," Christina called, waving her arms.

A man jumped out and jogged to Parker before the ambulance even finished rolling to a stop.

"Is he okay?" Christina said, half sobbing as she shifted her cramped legs without letting up the weight on Foxy's head. "Why did you take so long?"

The EMT didn't answer. He crouched over Parker while two others brought a stretcher.

Christina jumped when someone touched her shoulder. "It's been two minutes," a voice said. "You've done a good job, but I'm here to take over."

The voice belonged to a woman in coveralls with a

stethoscope around her neck. As she gently pushed Christina aside, Christina realized the woman was a vet. All of a sudden, the area seemed to be bustling with people.

"Hobble her legs," the vet ordered from her position at Foxy's head. "And take the saddle off. I don't think we can roll her over with it on."

A man undid one side of the girth, then tugged until the saddle was free. He passed it to Christina.

"At the count of three, pull."

It didn't take any time at all to roll Foxy over so that her legs were pointed in the other direction. As soon as Parker was unpinned, the EMTs crowded around him. Christina tried to see Parker's face as they shifted him to the stretcher, but there were too many people blocking the way.

"Okay, I'm going to let her up," the vet said, moving away from Foxy. Christina crossed her fingers as Foxy's head came off the ground and her front legs shot out. When the mare grunted and heaved herself up, everyone around her sighed in relief.

Then Parker cried out, "Is she all right?"

Christina set the saddle in the grass before running to where they were sliding Parker into the ambulance. His helmet was off, and eight webbed straps immobilized him from his ankles to his head. Parker's skin was gray, and tears were trickling down the sides of his dirt-streaked face.

"She's fine," Christina said, glancing back at Foxy,

who was looking around dazedly. "The vet's here."

Parker's eyes shifted as he watched one of the men try to lead Foxy forward. The mare held her left back hoof off the ground. "What's wrong with her leg?" Christina could hear his panic.

The vet came over and touched Parker's hand. "We're going to stabilize her leg with a splint, just like they've stabilized you. Then we'll take her to the clinic for X rays, and we'll tell you what we've found. We are not going to do *anything* without your permission. Do you understand?"

Parker tried to nod, but he couldn't. Christina could see his Adam's apple bob as he swallowed.

The vet smiled. "Now be a good patient so I can get back to mine." She nodded at the EMTs, then went back to Foxy.

A Jeep drove up as the ambulance was about to leave. Mr. Townsend jumped out from one side, and Ashleigh jumped out from the other. As soon as Christina saw her mother, she ran into her arms and burst into tears.

"It was horrible. Parker tried to jump, only Foxy ended up somersaulting over on him. I tried to stop them, but I couldn't."

Mr. Townsend got into the ambulance. Then it turned and drove across the field, going slower than it had come. The technical delegate who was in charge of the event asked Christina questions as the vet splinted Foxy's leg and loaded her onto a trailer that Christina hadn't even seen arrive.

"Do you think they're going to be all right?" Christina asked her mother.

"We'll just have to wait and see." Ashleigh squeezed Christina's shoulder. "I've seen worse crashes on the racecourse where everyone ended up healing fine. We have some of the best doctors and vets in the country."

When the TD closed her notebook, she looked at Christina. "Are you okay to ride?"

"I think so," Christina said, realizing she had finally stopped trembling.

The TD turned to Ashleigh. "And it's all right with you if she finishes?"

"I don't know yet. I have to think about it."

Christina's stomach sank as she looked at her mother. The TD seemed to understand, though.

"Cross-country will resume in five minutes. If you're going to ride, backtrack to where you can see jump nine and the judge will wave when it's time to start." Then the TD drove off in the Jeep, her walkie-talkie crackling as she gave instructions.

"Please, Mom?" Sterling was restless, bumping into Christina's shoulder. Christina gave the reins a tug to make her stand still.

Ashleigh put her hand under Christina's chin. "I'm afraid you'll get hurt."

When Christina pressed her lips together, trying not to cry, Ashleigh dropped her arm and looked away. Christina held her breath as she waited.

"The problem is," Ashleigh said, finally turning

back, "the rider side of me keeps arguing that it's up to you."

It took a few seconds for her words to sink in. "Thank you," Christina said, springing forward to give her mother a hug. Sterling jerked on the reins. When Christina turned, the mare was gazing down the field as though she was ready to run again.

"You'd better hurry before I change my mind," Ashleigh said.

But Christina was already putting her foot into the stirrup and swinging up into the saddle.

Ashleigh patted her boot. "Be careful."

Christina looked at the beaten-down grass where Foxy and Parker had lain. "Don't worry," she told her mother. "I will."

The last eight fences went smoothly, with Christina working doubly hard to keep Sterling focused. And when Sterling hesitated at the water jump, Christina clamped her legs with such determination that Sterling forged on.

As they cantered through the finish flags without any refusals or falls, Dylan and Katie cheered. The clean round was a hollow victory for Christina, though. She was too worried about Parker and Foxy to feel much of anything.

Dylan and Katie crowded around her, full of questions as she loosened Sterling's girth.

"Did you hear that Parker had an accident?" Katie asked. "They had to get him in an ambulance."

Christina undid the chin strap on her helmet. "I saw the whole thing."

"Where did it happen?" Dylan asked.

"At the jump that goes through the hay barn."

Katie's jaw dropped. "You jumped that?"

"No. It wasn't on our course. Parker passed me in the field, and the next thing I knew, he was jumping it." All of a sudden Christina was so tired that she could hardly talk.

"You can tell us about it later," Dylan said, taking Sterling's reins from her. "We've got to get back to the trailer to get ready for stadium anyway."

"You haven't gone yet?" The clock in her head was all muddled. It felt as though hours had passed since she'd left the starting box.

"They got a late start, and Parker's accident delayed them even more." Dylan put his hand on her shoulder. "You and Sterling looked good coming in."

Christina managed a smile. "Thanks."

An hour later everyone was talking about the accident. Christina was coming back from walking the stadium course when she overheard two women discussing it.

"He picked the wrong intermediate fence to try," one woman was saying. "Probably came at it too fast and the horse misjudged the distance."

"It's easy to do on that jump," the other woman said. "I had to trot my horse through it last year to give him time for his eyes to adjust to the change in light. On a bright day, you can't see anything in that barn at first."

Had Foxy wavered in front of the fence because she couldn't see it properly? But she'd jumped it anyway. Christina's stomach churned, and for a second she thought she was going to throw up. Had Foxy jumped because Parker asked her to? Because she had trusted he knew what he was doing?

Christina was quiet as she got Sterling ready to jump again. She'd never even thought twice about a horse's eyes adjusting from sunlight into shade. What else didn't she know? All of a sudden she understood why Mona had been so cautious about allowing her and Sterling to move up. By going in training level that day, Christina had put herself and her horse at great risk. It was only luck that she'd had a clean round in the cross-country.

"I don't know if I'm going to bother with stadium after all," she said when Dylan finished his jumping course. The clear round he'd ridden left him tied for second place in the novice division.

He turned in the saddle. "Why not? You're doing great so far."

Christina shrugged.

Dylan didn't say anything as he dismounted. Christina watched him run the stirrups up, tucking the leather straps through the irons. When he faced Christina, his eyes were serious.

"When I found out you moved Sterling up on your own, I thought it was dumb at first," he admitted.

"Maybe I was just mad that you hadn't talked to me about it."

Christina could feel her cheeks turning pink.

"But you've already done cross-country, and that's what Mona was worried about," Dylan continued. "Sterling can't get too out of control in stadium, and it's a tight course—just like we've been practicing at Mona's, only higher. Chances are Sterling won't hurt herself, even if she knocks down a rail or two, right?"

"I guess not."

Dylan squeezed her hand. "I know you're worried about Parker. We are, too," he said, motioning to Katie, who had been hanging back and listening. "But you know you'll be sorry if you don't keep going."

Christina sighed as she put her face against Sterling's big cheek. "I guess you're right. I'd better finish what I've started."

Christina felt as though she was on autopilot when she trotted Sterling into the stadium arena and halted in front of the judge. After saluting, she took a deep breath, chasing Parker and Foxy out of her head. Sterling needed 100 percent of her attention now.

They went from walk to canter in a single motion, with Sterling anxiously turning her head as she looked for the first fence. Christina's job was to keep the mare focused on one jump at a time, which was not an easy task in a ring full of brightly painted boards and panels.

She pointed Sterling toward the first flagged jump—a picket fence with three whiskey barrels in front that had been cut in half and turned into planters. Sterling's black-tipped ears flicked back and forth as they approached the yellow and red mums. She hesitated, sitting back on her haunches and switching canter leads, before taking off over the waving flowers. Sterling grazed the fence with a back hoof, but when Christina looked over her shoulder, the jump was still in place.

So far so good, she thought, guiding Sterling to the blue and white oxer. This time Sterling sailed over the poles with inches to spare, settling back into Christina's hands as they turned the corner for the in-and-out.

Thirteen jumps later, Christina faced Sterling's least favorite kind of fence—the liverpool. Sterling had jumped liverpools before, but they had been the fake kind with a boxed frame underneath that was painted blue to look like water.

This liverpool, however, was complete with water that sparkled like a mirror in the glare from the sun. It was one of those obstacles that was more scary than difficult for horses—just a three-foot jump made out of two poles and standards. If it weren't for the water underneath, it would be a simple schooling fence. But the water made all the difference, especially for Sterling, who had only recently started crossing brooks.

Sterling cantered up to the liverpool as though she were approaching a den of snakes, weaving from one side to the next as she changed leads. *Just like Foxy did before she fell*, Christina remembered.

Even though it wasn't unexpected, when Sterling put on the brakes and slid to a stop in front of the jump, Christina was almost thrown out of the saddle. She shoved herself off the pommel just as Sterling wheeled and dashed to the left. "Whoa," Christina said, shortening her reins and sitting back. When Sterling stopped, Christina could feel the mare's heart pounding under her legs.

Christina asked for a canter and made a tight circle back to the fence, determined to get Sterling over it. This time Sterling quit a full stride away from the edge of the water, popping off the ground with her front hooves when Christina slapped the mare's side behind her leg to urge her on.

This isn't working, Christina thought, suddenly close to tears. Sterling had given her so much already that day. She didn't want to ruin it by bullying her.

They stood for a few seconds while Christina took slow, deep breaths. Then she closed her legs on Sterling's sides and turned her away. "You can do this, you know," she said, her seat tilting out of the saddle as she reached up Sterling's neck to scratch behind her ear. Sterling turned her head to Christina and picked up a canter.

They were allowed to try the fence one more time. If Sterling refused again, they would be disqualified from the event. Christina sat back, asking Sterling to bend around her leg as though they were cantering a fifteen-meter circle in a dressage test. When Sterling responded, lifting her back and head while shortening her stride, Christina turned her to the water one last time.

She looked past the liverpool and saw Dylan standing by the fence. He straightened his back, lifting his chin as though he were the one riding. Christina lifted her chin even more, her seat molded to the saddle, her hands soft and coaxing as she concentrated on the canter. *Ignore the fence, just ride the canter. Dressage over fences.* The voice in her head was Mona's. Christina closed her eyes, rode the canter, and felt Sterling lift into the air. They were flying.

Sterling landed on the far side of the liverpool, kicking her heels up as she scooted away through the finish flags amid cheers from the crowd. "Good girl," Christina said over and over as she patted Sterling's neck.

Dylan met her at the gate. "You did it!" he yelled, waving his thumbs in the air.

"And it only took me three tries," Christina said, grinning. But she didn't care. Even though they wouldn't get a ribbon, Sterling had completed her first training-level event like a champion.

But what about Parker and Foxy?

Christina was brushing Sterling in the barn at Whitebrook after the event when her mother came in with news.

"I just talked to Clay Townsend. Parker broke his

arm and has a minor concussion, but the doctors say he's going to be fine."

Christina sagged in relief. The whole way back from the event, Parker had been on her mind. "I was afraid he was going to be paralyzed or something," she said, remembering the sickening sight of Foxy flipping over the jump, her light brown belly exposed to the sunlight as she fell on top of him.

"I know," her mother said. "I was thinking the same thing."

"How about Foxy? Did Mr. Townsend say if she's going to be okay?"

Her mother's face darkened. "They took a bone chip out of her hock. It'll take time before they can tell if she'll be sound again."

"Poor Foxy," Christina said, tucking her hand into the soft spot behind Sterling's front elbow. "Parker's going to be devastated if he can't ride her anymore."

"It'll be a shame, all right," her mom said. "It always breaks my heart to see a horse injured out of ignorance."

Christina started to protest. "But Foxy isn't like those horses with big knees at the auction, the ones whose trainers pushed them too hard. . . ." Her voice trailed off as she remembered the accident.

"Isn't she?" Her mother's voice was soft. "Foxy was trying to do as she was told. Parker didn't mean to hurt her with his inexperience, but she got hurt all the same."

Christina felt a lump forming in her throat. "It could just as easily have been me and Sterling."

"Oh, I don't know." Ashleigh put her arm around Christina and drew her close. "You don't have as many demons getting in the way of your judgment as Parker. I don't agree with what you did, going against Mona's wishes like that. But I think you weighed your decision pretty carefully. You may have been a little premature in moving Sterling up a level, but I don't think you were foolish."

Her mother's words made Christina feel a little better. "What do you mean by demons?" she said, wiping her hand across her nose.

Ashleigh hoisted herself onto Sterling's stall door before she answered. "Well, you know Parker hasn't had the kind of attention and support growing up that you've had."

"Tell me about it," Christina said. "I would hate it if you made me go away to school."

Her mother leaned over and tugged Christina's braid. "Not a chance." She straightened up again, wiggling sideways so that she could rest her shoulder against the post. "I get the feeling Parker does all these wild things because he's looking for attention."

"From his parents?" Christina wouldn't want to spend time with Lavinia and Brad Townsend. But then again, she might not feel that way if she was their daughter.

"From anyone." Her mother fiddled with her wedding ring. "From what I've heard, Parker was homesick in England. When he took the car and went to the racetrack, that was only one of the times he ran away from school."

Christina leaned against Sterling's warm barrel. Parker had run away? She'd never thought about it like that. Parker had made it sound as though he'd gone to the racetrack looking for a good time. But maybe that was just a cover-up. After all, when they'd walked the course, he admitted that he'd been homesick.

"I wonder why his parents even bothered having a kid," Christina fumed, thinking about Parker alone on weekends and holidays.

Ashleigh shook her head. "I bet poor Parker wonders that, too."

On Sunday morning after chores, Ashleigh took Christina to the hospital to see Parker. They asked Melanie if she wanted to come, but she said hospitals gave her the willies.

"Why did he have to stay overnight, anyway?" Christina asked as they waited for the elevator to take them to the third floor.

"I guess they wanted to keep him under observation, just in case," her mother answered. "Being knocked out is pretty serious stuff."

There were some people talking in the hall when they left the elevator. As Christina got closer, she recognized Parker's grandfather and parents.

"I hope nothing's wrong," her mother said with a worried frown.

Christina wondered, too. When they got closer, it was obvious that Parker's mother, Lavinia, was upset. Ashleigh took Christina's arm, motioning to her to slow down.

"Don't tell me to calm down. I can see for myself what that horse did to Parker, and I insist that she be destroyed."

Christina felt the blood drain from her face. When she looked at her mother, Ashleigh held her finger to her lips.

"Now, Lavinia. It wasn't the animal's fault," Clay Townsend said. "If Parker hadn't gone and jumped a fence that's not even on the course, nobody would have been hurt."

Brad cleared his throat. "And you can't just destroy a valuable animal like that. Even if she's lame, the mare could be sold for breeding."

He sounds like he doesn't even care about Foxy, Christina thought, *except for how much money he could get for her.*

"Well," Lavinia said, tugging at the bottom of her jacket as she turned and started down the hall, "at least I won't have to worry anymore about Parker being hurt. The Windsor-Huntington School in Connecticut has specific instructions not to let him have any contact with horses."

A chill ran down Christina's arms. They were going to send Parker away again.

11

"HELLO, ASHLEIGH," LAVINIA SAID WITH ALL THE WARMTH of a rock. She didn't even look at Christina as she swept by.

Brad Townsend would have ignored them, too, as he followed Lavinia down the hall, but his father took him by the arm. "Ashleigh, Christina," Mr. Townsend said, stopping beside them. "So good of you to come by and see Parker."

"Christina would have been here last night if I'd let her come," Ashleigh said. "We've been very anxious about how he's getting along."

"He's asleep now. Apparently the doctors and nurses had to keep waking him last night to check on him—concussion, you know—and now they've decided they can leave him alone." Mr. Townsend turned to his son, Brad. "Brad, we have this young lady to thank for helping during the accident. From what the EMTs said, she had the situation well under control when they arrived."

Christina smiled. Parker's grandfather was nice. He made her sound like a real hero.

"Yes. Well," Brad said, obviously eager to get away, "Lavinia and I have to wait for the doctor. I'll see you at the track," he said to Ashleigh.

Mr. Townsend shook his head at Brad's departing back. "You'll have to excuse my son," he said, turning to Ashleigh. "He's had a lot on his mind."

Yeah. I'll bet, thought Christina.

When Mr. Townsend said goodbye and followed Brad down the hall, Christina looked at her mother. "Can we at least see if he's awake?"

Ashleigh smiled. "Sure. We've come this far."

Christina found Parker's room at the end of the hall. She peeked around the corner, suddenly shy about being there.

Parker was lying with his eyes closed on the bed closest to the door. Christina glanced at the other bed, but it was empty.

"He's asleep," Christina mouthed to her mother before tiptoeing closer.

Except for the white cast that went from his fingers to his elbow and a purplish bruise on his forehead, Parker looked okay. Pale, maybe, but much better than the last time she'd seen him.

Christina jumped when his eyes opened. "Hi,

Parker." Her mind went blank and she couldn't think of anything else to say.

"Well, you're certainly looking good," Ashleigh filled in, going right up to the bed. "You had us all worried to death."

Parker managed a faint smile. "So I've heard."

"What kind of break is it?" Ashleigh asked.

"Simple fracture." He scowled at the cast.

Ashleigh nodded. "That's good. With your young bones, it should knit fast." Her mother knew a lot about fractures, having broken bones more times than Christina could remember from falling off racehorses.

Parker just lay there. It was strange seeing him so still. Christina kept expecting his face to light up, his mouth stretching into a grin as he said something outrageous. But his gray eyes stayed politely disinterested.

"Well," Ashleigh finally said, "it's good to see you. Come by the farm when you're feeling better." She turned to Christina. "I should stop in Mr. Hall's room to see how his hip is healing. I'll come and get you when I'm finished."

"Okay," Christina said, her eyes following her mother out of the room. It was nice of her to leave so that they could talk.

When Christina turned back again, Parker was staring out the window.

"Go ahead and say it." His voice sounded as though it belonged to another person.

"What?" Christina demanded, surprised.

"That I was stupid. That I ruined a horse I didn't deserve." He brushed his hand across his eyes, turning his head away as Christina sat down on the empty bed.

"It's too soon to tell if she's ruined," she said. "Anyway, it was an accident."

"It was stupid. I screwed up. I can't even be home for a month before my parents ship me off again."

"You heard?" Christina glanced at the open door.

"Of course I heard. How could I not hear them shouting about me? They've been doing it all my life." This time Parker didn't even try to hide the tears.

Christina stared at her sneakers, not sure what to say. "Well, at least Connecticut isn't as far away as England. I bet you'll be able to come home for holidays."

Parker snorted. "Big rah. I don't even have a home."

"Sure you do," Christina said, trying not to think about how empty and cold the Townsend house looked.

"You don't understand. How could you?" Parker's voice had gotten lower, as though the sound was coming from deep inside him.

Christina bit her tongue. He was right. She couldn't completely understand what things were like for him.

"Maybe next time I'll be lucky enough to break my neck," he said with a hollow laugh.

Christina remembered how afraid she'd been that he *had* broken his neck. "That's stupid," she said, jumping up. "If you don't care about yourself, at least think about Foxy."

"I am. She's better off without me." Parker shut his eyes and turned away.

"No, she's not," Christina said, touching his arm.

When Parker didn't move, Christina bit her lip and straightened, feeling foolish. She rubbed her thumbnail against her bottom lip as her mind scrambled for sense.

"Do you want me to make sure Foxy's doing okay?"

Had Parker nodded? Christina waited, but he didn't say anything.

"I guess I'd better go, then. Hope you feel better after you get some sleep." Christina hesitated before tiptoeing out of the room. When she looked back in, Parker still hadn't moved.

She felt horrible as she walked down the hall looking for her mother. Even though she had wanted to cheer him up, Christina had a terrible suspicion that she'd said all the wrong things. Maybe her mom would know what to do.

The last door before the nurses' station was a waiting room. Lavinia and Brad had made themselves at home on the sofa, flipping through magazines and sipping coffee from paper cups while Mr. Townsend perched in a straight chair watching the news. Christina walked past the door, then stopped. How could they just sit there when Parker needed them? She retraced her steps.

"Um, Mr. Townsend?" Christina said, standing in the doorway.

Both Brad and his father looked up expectantly. Lavinia stared at her coldly.

"Parker's awake, and he's really depressed," Christina said hesitantly.

"Depressed?" Lavinia said quizzically.

"He said he wishes he'd broken his neck." Christina's voice was shaking when she added, "I'm really worried about him."

"Aren't you sweet to be concerned," Lavinia said, her smooth, straight hair skimming her jaw as she smiled. "Frankly, we're all worried about him. That's why we're giving him a chance to make a fresh start."

"You are?" Christina said, brightening. Maybe she had misunderstood about the boarding school.

Brad put down his cup. "He's leaving for Connecticut next week. Maybe this time he'll think twice before going off half cocked on some lark."

Christina stared at Brad and Lavinia with their neatly pressed clothes and crossed legs. "Don't you even care about Parker?" she said before she could stop herself. "He's down there in his room crying. Crying in front of me, even, because you're going to send him away again."

"Parker, crying?" Brad looked a little less sure of himself.

"Yes." Christina was almost shouting. "Wouldn't you cry if everything you ever loved was being taking away from you?"

Lavinia tucked her hair behind one ear with a manicured hand. "I think you're being a little overdramatic."

"I don't think I am," Christina said, flushing at her own boldness. "Don't you see that Parker does crazy things for attention? If you ever listened to him, you'd know that Parker loves horses and riding more than anything. And if you try to take that away from him, I think he'll die."

Brad stood up. "Now see here—"

"Quiet." The older Mr. Townsend's voice boomed in the little room.

"But—" Brad started to say.

His father's bushy gray eyebrows shot up as he leaned forward, his hands gripping his knees. "But nothing. Sit down and listen," he ordered gruffly.

Christina wasn't used to hearing adults talked to in that tone of voice. She wondered if she should leave, but curiosity kept her feet rooted in the doorway.

Brad stood a few seconds more before shaking his head and sinking into a chair. He was acting just like a kid, Christina thought.

Mr. Townsend ran a hand along his jaw, pulling at the loose tanned skin before beginning.

"I've been standing by for years, watching the two of you try to mold that boy into someone he's not. Now, I understand why you want Parker to go into finance or law instead of racing, Lavinia. God knows the horse business is risky at best."

Lavinia straightened in her seat and smiled, looking smug.

"But the plain fact of the matter is that it's up to Parker to decide what he wants to do with his life. And I have a hunch that the more you try to keep him away from horses, the more he's going to want to be with them. I know I felt that way when I was his age. And I wouldn't say I've done too badly." Mr. Townsend sounded as if he was daring them to disagree.

Brad swallowed and answered, "No, sir."

Mr. Townsend nodded. "But I admit to making a few mistakes, and one of them was not speaking up when you got that fool notion to send the boy off to school. I never did cotton to the idea of other people raising him, and I should have said more against it."

Lavinia's eyes opened wide with indignation. "Are you telling us how to raise our son?"

"Darn right I am," Mr. Townsend said, slamming his hands down on his knees as he stood up. "Seeing as how you're doing such a poor job of it. I know Parker has a wild streak, but maybe that's because nobody's taking the time to put his energy to use." When Mr. Townsend straightened, Christina suddenly got the feeling she was seeing what Parker would look like someday. He took a couple of steps toward her, then turned back to Brad.

"You've got a son. It's about time you got to know him," he said, and strode toward Christina.

Christina backed out of the room as Mr. Townsend approached. Her heart pounded when he reached out, put his hand on the back of her arm, and steered her down the hall.

"And as for you, young lady," he began, his head fixed straight ahead as they walked.

Christina wondered if she should try to get away.

"You remind me of your mother when she was your age." Mr. Townsend glanced down. "Spunky."

Christina smiled. Spunky? That didn't sound too bad.

"There you are," Ashleigh said, coming out of Parker's room and walking down the hall toward them. "I was wondering where you were."

"She was stirring up trouble." Mr. Townsend winked at Christina. "About time somebody did."

Ashleigh's brow was furrowed as she watched Mr. Townsend disappear into Parker's room. When she turned back and started to speak, Christina jumped in first.

"I'll tell you about it on the way home."

It took two days for Christina to work up the nerve to call Parker. She didn't know if he was still mad from her visit.

"Parker Townsend was released on Monday," a crisp voice informed her when she dialed the hospital.

"Released?" Christina repeated. "You mean he's home now?"

"I'm sorry, but I'm not allowed to give out that information."

"Well, thanks anyway," Christina said. She put her

finger on the disconnect button, thinking, *Now what am I supposed to do?* She didn't want to risk calling him at home in case Lavinia or Brad answered. Christina had the feeling she was the last person they'd want to talk to. Not that she wanted to talk to them, either.

On Wednesday in algebra she asked Cassidy if her brother, Campbell, had mentioned seeing Parker in school.

"No, why?"

When Christina told her what she'd heard in the hospital, Cassidy was sympathetic. "They're going to send him away again? Those creeps." She promised she'd ask Campbell as soon as she got home.

On Thursday after homeroom, Cassidy met her in the hall with bad news. "Campbell says Parker hasn't been in school all week."

"Maybe he had to stay home because of the concussion," Christina said, trying to be optimistic. Even Brad and Lavinia wouldn't ship him off without giving him a chance to say goodbye, would they?

12

On Friday afternoon Melanie wrestled the phone from Christina.

"For Pete's sake. *I'll* call the Townsends. The worst they can do is hang up on me." She wrinkled her nose before adding, "And that's a lot better than hearing you wonder about Parker all weekend."

Christina put her ear close to the receiver so that she could listen, too. The phone rang three times before it was answered.

"Hello?"

Christina would recognize that syrupy voice anywhere. *It's Lavinia,* she mouthed to Melanie.

"Hi. Can I speak to Parker?"

"Who is calling?"

Melanie grimaced before saying, "This is Melanie Graham."

"I don't believe I know you, Melanie." Lavinia paused, waiting.

"Uh," Melanie said, fighting back the giggles, "you know my aunt and uncle, Ashleigh Griffen and Mike Reese."

The silence on the other end was so thick that Christina thought Lavinia must have hung up.

"Ah, yes," Lavinia said finally, drawing out the *s* sound. "Well, Parker is not available right now. Good day."

Melanie held the receiver out as though it had hissed at her. "She hung up on me. What charm school did she flunk out of?"

Christina wasn't surprised. "See what I mean? Poor Parker."

On Saturday morning there was frost on the grass at the edge of the field. Christina and Dylan rode bareback side by side, their blue-jeaned legs brushing when Sterling stepped into Dakota to avoid a rock.

"Sorry." Christina pushed her calf against Sterling's barrel to move her back over, but Dylan caught her eye.

"I don't mind," he said, and Christina blushed as they walked along.

Christina had been doing a lot of thinking this past week about how she could like Dylan so much and still like Parker, too. Melanie said it was because Parker was dangerous and sophisticated. Christina thought her cousin had been reading too many romance novels.

Christina sighed. She usually loved these early Saturday morning rides. But even Sterling's muscles rippling under her seat and the pungent smell of damp leaves couldn't chase her worries away.

"So . . . did you find out yet if Parker's going to stay in Kentucky?" Dylan asked, breaking the peaceful stillness.

"No." Christina wondered if Dylan had been reading her mind.

"Why don't we ride over to his house and ask?" Dylan suggested.

"His parents would probably sic their dogs on us." Christina said.

Dylan didn't seem too worried. "What kind of dogs?"

"I don't know," she said, laughing in spite of herself. "It's just an expression."

At that point Sterling's head jerked up. The mare snorted as a small brown rabbit zipped across their path.

Dylan made fun of the way Sterling snorted loudly, crouching down as she slunk past the place where the rabbit had disappeared. "How can a horse brave enough to jump training-level cross-country fences be so scared of a little rabbit?"

"Sterling doesn't have time to be scared over cross-country," Christina said. She stuck out her tongue at him before shortening her reins. "Want to canter?"

Dylan nodded, pressing his hiking boots into Dakota's sides. Sterling leaped forward before Christina even asked, matching Dakota stride for stride.

"If she shies, I'm road kill," Christina said, curling her long legs around Sterling's dappled barrel. The mare felt even more powerful than usual when there wasn't a saddle between them.

Christina and Dylan raced across the field. It was only when they slowed down to turn onto the trail by Whisperwood Farm that Christina remembered Parker again. She looked at the place where he and Foxy had appeared the first time she saw him on the mare, all fired up and happy. Parker never had gotten a chance to go out hacking with them.

Christina pushed herself back from Sterling's withers. "Let's stop at Samantha's for something to drink," she said. "My mouth is all dry."

Dylan rested one hand on Sterling's neck as he leaned over and gave Christina a quick kiss. "Feels okay to me," he teased, grinning at her surprised face. They were only walking, but Christina had to grip Sterling's mane to keep from falling off.

When they got to Whisperwood, Christina could hear someone whistling inside the barn. Probably Tor, she thought. She slipped off Sterling's back.

"Hello," Christina sang out as she led Sterling out of the bright sunshine and onto the concrete aisle. A couple of horses stuck their heads over the stall doors and whinnied. One of the horses was a bay with a white star.

"Foxy?" As Christina came closer, Parker's head appeared, too.

"The one and only," he said, a grin spreading across his narrow face.

"What are you guys doing over here? I was afraid you were in Connecticut," Christina said.

"I almost was. You should have heard the row."

Dylan came up behind them. "So you're not going?"

Was it Christina's imagination, or did Dylan sound disappointed?

"No." Parker face was shining. "I made a pact with my grandfather."

"What kind of pact?" Christina asked as Parker rested his cast on Foxy's back.

"If I stay out of trouble, he'll keep my parents off my back about riding." Parker ran the brush down Foxy's neck before adding, "I'm not sure, but I think he threatened to cut off Dad's money if they try to send me away to school again." Christina could see his jaw tighten, but when he turned, he was smiling again. "I'm going to be a working student for Tor and Samantha. Not that I can do much until I get this off," he added, waving his cast.

"A working student?" Dylan's eyes lit up. "I've always wanted to do that."

"Me too," Christina added. She and Dylan had both talked about apprenticing themselves to a big-time event rider after they finished high school.

"It was one of the conditions," Parker said. "My grandfather says if I'm going to event, I should do it right. He's the one who set it up so Tor and Samantha would teach me."

Foxy stuck her nose over the door to sniff Sterling. "So how's Foxy?" Christina scratched the bay's nose. "She's looking better than I expected."

"I think she likes it here. It's quieter than Townsend Acres."

"What's that on her chest?" Christina grimaced at the grapefruit-sized lump just above the mare's legs.

Parker ran his fingers gently over it. "A hematoma from when she fell. It's full of blood from the bruising, but it will go away gradually."

The picture of Foxy lying still on the ground flashed into Christina's head. "Did she knock herself out when she fell?"

"The vet doesn't think so. She was probably just winded."

"Ouch," Christina said. She knew what that felt like.

Dylan spoke up. "How about her hock?"

Parker frowned. "It will be a couple of months before we know if the nerves will be okay. Samantha showed me some massage I can do to increase the blood supply to her leg, though. We're hoping it will help her heal faster."

Christina stared at the swollen hock. It was an ugly reminder of the accident.

"I wish I could take it all back," Parker said sud-

165

denly, as though he were reading their minds. "I'm going to make it up to her, you know."

Foxy rested her muzzle on Parker's shoulder, nuzzling his ear.

"She doesn't look like she's holding a grudge," Dylan said kindly.

Christina looked at him in surprise. Did this mean that he wasn't mad at Parker anymore, either?

Parker's Adam's apple bobbed as he reached under Foxy's neck and scratched her ear. "Thanks," he said. "I don't ever want to be responsible for hurting a horse again."

"Well, if it isn't the rabble-rouser," a gravelly male voice boomed behind them, making Christina jump. She turned and saw a tall gray-haired figure striding down the aisle. "Hello, Mr. Townsend," Christina said politely.

"Hey, Grandpa," Parker said, letting himself out of Foxy's stall. "What are you doing here?"

"I need an excuse to see my grandson?" Mr. Townsend pulled Parker to him in a one-armed hug.

"Seriously, though," Parker said, worry crossing his face.

"Seriously," Mr. Townsend echoed, dropping his arm. "I got this in the mail today." He drew a sheet of paper out of his breast pocket and handed it to Parker. Christina watched his face as he read.

Parker looked up, puzzled. "It's an auction. What does this have to do with me?"

"I thought we could go to it, find a nice young Thor-

oughbred for you to work while your mare is healing."
Mr. Townsend pulled at his chin. "That is, if you're stay-
ing out of trouble."

Parker nodded his head. "You can count on it, sir."

"Good."

"But I don't want another horse," Parker said, handing the sheet back.

Mr. Townsend's eyebrows shot up. "I thought you
wanted to be an event rider."

"I do, sir." Parker reached up to stroke Foxy. "But I
want to wait for Foxglove. I can work Samantha and
Tor's horses for now."

Mr. Townsend's hand rested briefly on his grandson's head as he studied him. Christina got the feeling
he was pleased by Parker's answer. "Well, then. Let's
see this massage business you're trying."

Both of them disappeared into Foxy's stall. Christina caught Dylan's eye and tilted her head toward the
door. "We'll see you later, Parker," she called.

"When your arm is healed, maybe you can borrow a
horse and go out hacking with us," Dylan offered.

"That would be great." Parker waved, then turned
back to his grandfather.

"Thanks," Christina said as she and Dylan led their
horses out of the barn.

Dylan looked puzzled. "For what?"

"For being a nice guy."

*   *   *

167

Christina rode her bike over to Mona's early Sunday morning, when she was pretty sure no one else would be around yet. It was the first chance she'd had to talk to her trainer alone.

"Long time no see," Mona said when she answered the door. "Come on in. I was about to make some hot chocolate."

Christina lifted Bart, one of Mona's cats, off a kitchen chair while Mona filled the kettle. "Did you hear about me and Sterling?" Christina said, getting straight to the point.

Mona leaned against the counter. "I heard you took her training level, if that's what you mean."

Christina looked at the Formica table. This was going to be harder than she thought. "I know I shouldn't have gone without your permission." She expected Mona to agree with her, but when she didn't say anything, Christina looked up.

Mona was looking at her thoughtfully. "Maybe it's time you branched out a little and worked with someone else."

"No!" Christina said, springing to her feet. She'd thought Mona would yell. It never crossed her mind that Mona would refuse to teach her anymore.

Mona laughed. "Don't look at me like that. I'm not suggesting you switch teachers because I'm mad at you."

"You're not mad?"

"Well," Mona said thoughtfully, "I was angry at

first. But when I got to thinking about it, I realized that eight years is a lot of time to spend with one instructor—even one as good as I am," she added with a smile.

Christina's mouth trembled.

"Come here," Mona said, putting an arm around Christina and looking her straight in the eye. "Part of the reason you've been taking lessons from me instead of your mom all these years is because Ashleigh thought she might hold you back for fear you would get hurt. It's hard to teach your own little girl." Mona paused. "And now I'm wondering if I've been doing the very same thing."

Christina sniffed. "You mean you think Sterling and I are ready for training level after all?"

Mona raised her eyebrows as she nodded. "Of course, there aren't any guarantees in eventing or anything else to do with horses. Even the best riders get hurt sometimes. But to answer your question, yes. I think you and Sterling have shown that you're ready to move on, and I think Samantha Nelson would be the logical person to give you what you need. I hardly have time to teach all my students, much less keep up with higher-level eventing."

"But what about Katie and Dylan?" Christina couldn't imagine riding lessons without her friends.

"I don't know whether Katie's ever going to want to leave the novice level of eventing," Mona said. "As for Dylan, he'll have to decide for himself." She gave Christina a squeeze before turning away to get the kettle. "Just think about what I've said. You can always come back for an occasional lesson if you get homesick for my abuse," she teased.

Christina's head was spinning as she rode back home. It made her sad to think about not riding over to Mona's for lessons with her friends anymore. Still, the prospect of training with an experienced event rider like Samantha was exciting. She had to admit she'd been envious when Parker had told her about working with Samantha and Tor. Maybe Dylan would want to ride at Samantha's, too.

But even if Dylan didn't want to take lessons at Whisperwood Farm, Parker would be there. Riding with him had always been fun. Christina sighed. She had the feeling that life was going to be a little more complicated now that Parker was here to stay.

Christina turned her bike onto Whitebrook's driveway, smiling as Sterling trotted over to the pasture fence to greet her.

"Come on, girl," she said, scratching Sterling's silver dapples. "Let's go for a ride."